Praise for

CLUES *to the* UNIVERSE

"In this touching debut, Li masterfully weaves
the tale of Ro and Benji, two friends bound by their love of
a space comic that leads them on their own adventures in search
of Benji's missing father. *Clues to the Universe* shines with
larger-than-life characters the power of science, and
a friendship greater than any force in the universe.
Heartwarming, imaginative, timeless!"
—KATIE ZHAO, author of *The Dragon Warrior*

"*Clues to the Universe* reminds us that we're all made of stardust,
and—regardless of how little we feel, and how many losses we
face—that magic lurks in us, waiting to be tapped into. It is an
achingly beautiful and thoughtfully written debut that will find
its way into the heart of readers seeking heart, hope, and a sense
of wonder as they navigate family, friendship, and the world
around them." **—KARUNA RIAZI,** author of *The Gauntlet*

"With an engaging voice and perfectly lovable characters,
Clues to the Universe is a heart-filling journey
of hope, healing, and friendship."
—CINDY BALDWIN,
author of *Where the Watermelons Grow* and *Beginners Welcome*

"Christina Li's *Clues to the Universe* is a triumphant story of
friendship, loss, and the journey of finding your place
in the world (and among the stars). A reminder that we
sometimes have to travel great distances to find the secrets
of what makes life beautiful. A remarkable debut!"
—PABLO CARTAYA, award-winning, bestselling author
of *The Epic Fail of Arturo Zamora*

CLUES
to the
UNIVERSE

CHRISTINA LI

Quill Tree Books
An Imprint of HarperCollins Publishers

ISBN 978-0-06-300888-5

Typography by Ray Shappell
20 21 22 23 24   PC/LSCH   10 9 8 7 6 5 4 3 2 1

First Edition

To Katia

CHAPTER ONE
RO

THE LAST TIME I watched a rocket launch, I learned that there is no sound in space.

Over the tinny sounds of the TV, it had sounded like someone was ripping a sheet of paper right next to my ear. But I knew that to the people standing there, wearing soundproof earmuffs with their T-shirts and sandals, it was louder than that. I'd tried to think of the loudest things I knew: the washing machines at the laundromat on the corner of the street near my dad's favorite breakfast place, my neighbor's lawn mower that growled to life early every Saturday morning, the firecrackers that the kids down the street set off on the Fourth of July, starting a chain of events that led to a crew of wailing fire trucks and a furious army of neighborhood moms, all swarming around one of the kids' porches. In that order.

But none of that compared to the space shuttle.

I knew how big it was: a quarter million pounds and a hundred and eighty-four feet long. A hundred and eighty-four feet equaled almost thirty-seven Ros, if you lined me all up from head to toe. Or almost-but-not-quite thirty-one Dads, since he was six feet tall. It was like hurling a big building into the sky. Except the shuttle was even larger than the biggest building I'd ever seen.

So last November 11, when I made myself a bowl of Cocoa Puffs and sat in my living room, I watched the *Columbia* launch into the air with clouds of fire and smoke, loud enough that the people watching (who seemed like tiny ants compared to the *Columbia*) clapped their hands over their fuzzy earmuffs and stared on in awe. As I spooned bites of soggy cereal into my mouth and wondered aloud if the rocket was loud enough to be heard from the moon, Dad replied that no, sound didn't exist in outer space. Or on the moon, for that matter.

What I've learned since then is that there is no sound in space because outer space is made of a great big nothing. A vacuum. But here, sounds consist of little tiny invisible sound particles bumping into each other until they reach someone's ear, like the people at the grocery store or in a busy train station.

Or like the kids in the hallways of my new school with its narrow hallways and too-many windows, bumping from friend to friend until they reached their classrooms.

As I glanced through the window of the library door of that new school, with its shiny stacks of books and its buzzing crowds of students I didn't know, who'd gathered around the small TV on a cart to watch the launch, I wanted that kind of silence. I had done my speaking for the day—mostly to tell the school secretary, who wore purple lipstick and stared at me through beady eyes, that I was the new student at Roosevelt Middle School, and to tell Mom, who was nervously chewing her piece of mint gum and twisting the ring around her finger and wearing her Fancy Realtor Jacket when she hugged me tight, that yes, Mom, I would be all right on my first day here.

All I wanted to do right now was sit in the library and count to ten. Or a hundred.

Today was August 30. It had been 276 days since the last time I watched a rocket launch, and I was now three minutes late for my next class.

It had been 276 days since I last sat down with Dad, hugging a bowl of Cocoa Puffs in front of the TV, and decided that I, too, would build a rocket. And what I now thought about was the half-built rocket sitting in the closet of my bedroom, and how Dad would never be here to watch a shuttle launch with me again.

CHAPTER TWO

BENJI

ALIENS WERE REAL: I was sure of that.

What was harder to figure out was how to prove it to Amir when he was all the way across the country.

It had been way easier when he was here. I'd practically memorized the bike path to his house, with its chipped white paint and the rusted iron weather vane and all the weird garden gnomes that the previous owner had left behind. Two days before the Karimi family stuffed every last blanket, picture frame, and silverware set into their Ford station wagon and bundled up their living room rug, I biked over for the last time and Amir's mom let me have some gaz they'd been saving up. We settled on the front steps of his porch. I bit into the sticky Persian candy, running my tongue over the pistachio nougat.

I whipped out a folded newspaper article from my pocket.

It had crinkled to the shape of my jeans, but I smoothed it out. "UFO Sighting in Cleveland by Teenagers."

"Likely some prank," Amir said. "They probably made it up to get some attention."

"But what if it's real?" I pressed. "Something like this was in the *New York Times* a couple of years ago." Mom read that every Sunday morning—if only to skim the news to do the crosswords, which she said calmed her. "In Berkeley, too."

Amir shrugged, polishing off his gaz. "Maybe it's a Russian conspiracy."

"Come on," I said, holding up the half-eaten candy. "Think about it. What if aliens came here? They've probably never tried something like this before."

"A lot of people haven't tried it," Amir said. "There are probably two Iranian families in all of Sacramento."

"Or Red Vines," I said. "And what if they haven't seen trees before? Do you think they'll know how to talk to humans?"

"Wouldn't that be a little far-fetched?"

"Not in *Spacebound*."

Amir met my eyes and grinned. "Can't believe I got you hooked on those comics."

"I mean, it's not a bad story. And I really want to know what happens to that spaceship."

Amir stood up. "If a new *Spacebound* issue comes out, send it to me, all right? Just in case I can't get it in New Haven."

"On it." I stuffed the newspaper back in my pocket. "I'll send you some Red Vines too. I'll put together a survival package."

Amir laughed. "Sounds good, Ben Franklin."

Amir liked to call me Ben Franklin, mostly because Benjamin Franklin was his favorite American historical figure, and I was the only other Benjamin Amir knew. There wasn't any other resemblance. I mean:

Benjamin Franklin, founding father of our country.

Benjamin Burns, founder of our school's two-person art club. Down to one person now that the other member was moving to New Haven, Connecticut.

No matter how many times Amir had pointed out New Haven on a map, telling me to memorize its latitude and longitude, or explained that that was where Yale was, a fancy college with a hospital where his baba had just gotten a job, I just couldn't picture this place. Amir had said it was in the Ivy League, and I didn't really know what that meant. Maybe there was a lot of ivy there?

I could already imagine it as the cover of a comic— monstrous ivy vines snaking across a city.

Evil Plantlike Creature Attacks a Small Town!!! Who Will Save the Civilians??

A character emerges from the roots—

Okay, maybe New Haven wasn't like that. But it was far, for sure.

Really, really far.

As in, approximately 2,800 miles of biking distance.

"Send me some comics anyway," Amir said. "And tell me if a UFO comes, too."

I grinned. "Course I will."

Now, on the first day of school, I stared down at the letter I was writing. Things really had been so much easier with Amir around. If there were an alternate universe in which Dr. Karimi hadn't moved his family all the way across the country, Amir would have been here making science class more fun. Or at least bearable. Instead, I had to overhear Drew Balonik and his friends bragging loudly about setting off fireworks on the Fourth of July.

"It was *neat*," Drew was saying. "Until that old guy Voltz down the street came out and went totally ballistic."

"I've heard he's like that, though," one of Drew's friends said. "Voltz is a total spaz. People say he has fits sometimes. And that he doesn't like people. Jenny tried to shoplift at his store once and he caught her, and now she won't even go near that block."

I gritted my teeth and sketched an alien in the corner of the paper as the teacher started calling attendance.

"Benjamin Burns."

I looked up at Mr. Devlin, wondering whether to correct him or not. They called him Toothpick because he resembled one, with narrow, long legs and a seemingly even longer face. His head was smooth and shiny, like a gumball.

I cleared my throat. "Benji," I croaked out, just as the classroom door slammed open.

A girl in a faded blue-and-white windbreaker came into the room.

Drew Balonik and his firework-launching friends in the back went silent for a moment to stare. One of them snickered and then turned it into a weak cough. Drew raised his eyebrows and leaned in to whisper to one of his friends.

I had honestly, positively never seen her before in my life.

She brushed frizzy hair back from her face, scanned the class with a wide-eyed stare, and then walked straight to the only open seat in the class. Which happened to be the other seat at my table.

She didn't say a word.

Toothpick looked back at the class as if nothing had happened. "Benjamin Burns?"

"Here," I mumbled. I turned back to my drawing. As Toothpick went over things about labs and goggles and safety precautions, I pulled out the latest *Spacebound* issue and copied one of the planets so the alien would be sitting on something. While I was trying to sneak colored pencils under my notebook, I saw how the new girl was stacking notebooks one on top of another, reorganizing her folders, and then reshuffling them. Instead of a bracelet, she wore a huge black watch. It looked out of place on her wrist. I began drawing freckles on the alien face.

What I hadn't realized, when I reached up to sneak

another colored pencil, was that the new girl had carefully placed an open thermos right next to my elbow.

I knocked it over, the full metal bottle making a dull thud on the table. Water spilled everywhere. I grabbed the letter out of the puddle and pushed my folder and notebook to the floor, making an even bigger mess.

Heads turned. Two colored pencils bounced on the floor. Toothpick stopped talking.

The new girl stared at the mess.

I swear, my face was a million degrees. I slunk over to the counter and grabbed a bunch of paper towels and cleaned up the mess. I snuck a glance at the girl. She was lining up my colored pencils in the order of the rainbow. Red-orange-yellow-green-blue-purple.

"I'm sorry," she burst out. "I just didn't—"

"It's fine," I mumbled.

We didn't exchange another word for the rest of class. When the bell rang, I scooped up my purple folder and bolted for the door, clutching my half-finished letter and wishing I could just keep drawing freckles on this alien until the day was over.

It wasn't until after six more classes—after I was waiting in the school pick-up lane—that I realized my comic book was missing.

Here are some of the reasons to freak out about losing the latest issue of *Spacebound*:

1. Captain Gemma Harris, the main character, was left stranded on the dust-covered planet with her broken spaceship after being chased by evil bounty hunters across the galaxy, and I was dying to find out if she and her trusty spacepup had escaped.

2. I'd spent sixty cents buying the latest issue of these comics last week, along with another three dollars on a carton of Red Vines and stamps to send my letters, and I wasn't sure I could afford any more, especially now that Mom cut my allowance down.

3. It was the key to finding my missing dad.

All of those reasons, actually. But mostly number three.

CHAPTER THREE
RO

SOMETIMES IF YOU follow a certain set of rules just right, you can get the exact same results every time. Like how if I followed my nana's chocolate chip cookie recipe just right, I'd end up with perfectly chewy cookies. If I built the radio kit exactly like how the pictures showed me, I had a small but perfectly functional radio that played Dad's favorite rock radio station when we turned it on. And if you look at a right triangle and add up the squares of the shorter sides, the sum always equals the square of the third.

Dad always said that all someone needed to do to make a friend was to smile and to talk to them. I always thought there were more steps involved with this plan. But it seemed easy enough for him—he could talk to anyone and everyone. He once chatted with a cashier long enough for his mint-chip ice cream to melt.

The thought of talking to a single person—much less a hundred and twenty—made my stomach flip. Some people were much better at talking. Like the girl who sat next to me in art class on the first day and had shiny straight brown hair with lots of colorful clips in it and one of those big smiles. I only had a faded white hair tie that I used to rein in my frizzy hair. Half the time it was a losing battle. Over watercolors she told me I had a cool name and asked me where I came from, and when I said that I didn't move houses, only schools, she shrugged and said, "Huh." She snuck a piece of Hubba Bubba gum under the desk and told me not to tell Mr. Keanan, and when his back was turned, she blew a big pink bubble. But she smiled at me and told me her name was Charlotte Wexler, and that was more than anyone else who'd sat next to me had done. She also had a nice smile. Her nails were painted bright blue.

I'll be friends with her.

At lunch I saw Charlotte's blue backpack from across the lunchroom. I walked up to her, my bag lunch in hand, and smiled.

"Can I sit here?"

Charlotte stared up at me, her green eyes wide. I tucked a strand of hair behind my right ear and straightened up. The girl sitting next to her laughed into her peanut butter sandwich. Mostly they just stared.

"Sorry, what?"

I stretched my smile wider. "I'm Ro. Remember?"

The guys whispered around the table. I recognized one of them as the kid who'd set off the fireworks. He was in my science class, too.

He snickered. "Hey, Char, who is she?"

Charlotte swallowed. She shot Fireworks Boy a look. "Some girl I met in art class." She smiled back at me, but it didn't reach her eyes. "Yeah, of course you can sit here."

And then she went right back to talking to her friends.

I'd brought a baggie of M&M's that day, and when I got up to get a napkin, half the candy was missing by the time I got back. I felt hot and itchy, sitting on the edge of their table. But I didn't want to have to do this all over again tomorrow with someone new, so I stayed put and observed.

Dad always said that a good scientist made observations. I observed how Charlotte's friends all had sparkly hair clips and painted their nails in all kinds of bright shades. I saw how Fireworks Boy, who was actually named Drew, stole a kid's peanut butter cup.

Here are some other observations I'd made about Roosevelt Middle School since I'd gotten there that morning.

- Charlotte Wexler had two kinds of smiles: the one when Drew Balonik was talking to her, where she smiled extra big, and the smile she gave me.

- Every girl in the school seemed to have the same sparkly barrettes.

- The boy next to me in science just drew through the entire class. After he finished up what looked like a letter, he pulled out a sketchbook. I saw mostly planets. And explosions. He had a two-page spread of the map of the US that he'd torn out of some magazine and scribbled on. He'd drawn the same cartoon person all over it. On the right-hand side he'd written *Places He Could Be?* with arrows pointing to all the versions of the cartoon person.

- The locker room after gym class smelled like strawberries. Not the fresh kind of strawberries from a grocery store, but the fake kind that smelled too sweet and made me slightly sick.

It was in those locker rooms that I overheard Charlotte. I'd been looking for my clothes for the past ten minutes. They weren't in the locker I'd put them in.

"She just *put* her stuff in my locker," Charlotte was saying, her voice sharp. She and her friend were standing on the other side of the lockers, leaning over the sink and swiping on mascara. "I couldn't stand it. I just shoved her clothes somewhere else."

I got a tight feeling in my gut. I had no idea that we were given assigned lockers for gym class. I frantically scanned every locker around me. They all looked the same.

There. My jeans were peeking out.

"Her pants always look like they're about to fall off." It was the voice of Holly, the girl who sat next to Charlotte at the lunch table. "Does she shop at Goodwill or something?"

"She probably got sweat all over my new shirt."

There was a pause. Holly asked, "What *is* she?"

"What?"

"I mean, she looks kind of Japanese or something. But I can't really tell. Her eyes look different."

My cheeks burned. I thought about staying quiet and waiting for them to leave, but I didn't want to hear them talking anymore. I slammed my locker door shut, a little too hard.

Charlotte's voice dropped to a whisper. "What was that?"

I walked right past them, through the sickly-sweet strawberry-scented perfume cloud, and out the door.

I usually liked informing people about things. I informed my English teacher the other day about a missing apostrophe. I liked reminding Mom to take her daily vitamins and to not forget her keys. I could have faced Charlotte and Holly and told them that I was exactly half Chinese, a quarter Scottish, and a quarter Irish, but my face felt all hot and my throat closed up and I couldn't get the words out.

When I got home, I poured myself a cup of milk and grabbed some Cocoa Puffs. I leaned back in my seat and turned the TV on. They were replaying the launch I'd seen that morning. Instinctively, I reached inside my backpack to pull out my purple folder and knew that something was wrong.

It was the wrong folder.

I set my backpack down and sat, the carpet prickly against the backs of my knees. The notes I'd scribbled down during the launch were gone, replaced by a thick wad of creased drawing sheets, watery colored-pencil stains, and three comic books so well-worn that the pages were fraying at the corners.

How could I not have noticed? We had the same exact kind of purple folder. One labeled, one not. One that was mine, and one that belonged to the boy next to me in science class who'd scowled at me and then knocked my water bottle all over my Ticonderoga pencils.

"Ro?"

Mom emerged from the room behind me. It wasn't quite a room, really. It was more like a closet. But Mom had stuffed the shelves full of her books—alphabetized by me—and crammed the single window ledge with her growing collection of potted pants. It was her Sun Library—Sunbrary for short—because the one window took up approximately half of the wall.

She came over and folded me in a hug. She'd taken off her Stiff Fancy Work Jacket and instead wore a faded sweater. She smelled like the lavender lotion she always used.

"You were so quiet when you came home. I almost didn't notice you. You found your way around okay, baobao?"

I nodded into Mom's shirt. I looked up. "How was work?"

"Not bad," she said. A few stray wisps that had escaped from her short ponytail caught the light and turned her jet-black hair gold. "My client brought me cookies today." She pushed a box of lumpy and homemade-looking snicker-doodles toward me. I bit down into the soft cinnamon sweetness.

At least Mom didn't have to change schools.

As if reading my mind, Mom said quickly, "Look, if you ever want to switch back, we can always go back to the Day School. I mean, it's probably only their first week—"

"It's fine, Mom." I looked up. "School's good. I promise."

If I really wanted to stay at the Country Day School, Mom would have written the check without hesitating. Mom had only told me that going to a public school would make things easier. But I knew what easier meant. Easier meant being able to buy groceries without worrying, even if Mom still used every single coupon she could get her hands on out of principle. Easier meant Mom not having to work more hours. Easier meant fewer SpaghettiOs dinners and more stir-fry.

17

And the public school wasn't that different from the Day School. Other than the fact that there were no uniforms. And the fact that the number of kids in my grade went from thirty-two to a hundred and twenty.

Which meant four times the number of people in the halls during passing period, all wearing different-colored shirts. And four times the noise, the sound particles wildly oscillating within the narrow halls. People tossed paper airplanes across hallways. There were thirty kids in my science class. The purple-folder boy scribbled drawings through the entire class, and the teacher never noticed.

Mom suddenly looked up. "I almost forgot. I have to water my orchids."

As she hurried back into her Sunbrary, I wandered into the kitchen. Towels and dirty plates were scattered everywhere. Mom tended to pile dishes in the sink, and without Dad here, the plates just sat there. I started organizing the towels by color.

Blue on top of red.

Red on top of yellow.

Yellow on top of green.

Green on top of white.

Order calmed me down. It seemed like I was always cleaning up after Mom, but I didn't mind. It made me less nervous when books were put neatly on shelves and towels were color-coordinated. Organizing made for a good Next Best Step.

It was something I'd perfected over the last few months since That Night in March with the terribly white hospital walls and curtains and Dad's heart beeping in the wrong rhythm because a drunk driver had swerved into the wrong lane. I remembered the smell of antiseptic making me sick and pattern of the tiles on the hospital floor. I remembered the nurse who hugged me tight and said, "I'm so sorry, sweetheart," and Mom collapsed and cried more than I ever remembered her crying while I could only numbly stare at those tiles and at a pamphlet lying on the chair.

Grief: The Next Steps.

As if I could even think of taking more than one step.

So I made up the Next Best Step.

What was the best thing I could do right now, in this situation, to try to make things even a tiny bit better?

They were small things. Like hugging Mom. Or eating an entire chocolate chip cookie. Or wearing Dad's big digital watch on my left wrist and not taking it off except for showers. Or making sure I had tissues by my bed when I needed them. Mom's Next Best Steps filled up her Sunbrary and spilled over to the kitchen. At first she just took care of aloe plants, and then it was English ivy. Now she'd gone on to orchids. She also talked to her parents for hours on the phone on weekends, speaking in a rapid-fire mix of Mandarin and English.

Now, after an entire summer of doing little things, I'd moved on to bigger things, like taking inventory of the house. It was soothing, in a way. Plus, if I properly recorded the things we had in the house, they'd never be lost again.

I closed the door behind me and sat on my bedroom floor next to a cardboard box. I grabbed a legal pad and a ballpoint pen, and opened up the box.

For a long time after That Night, Dad's things went untouched. It was weird, seeing his jacket lie across the chair as if he were going to come back and retrieve it, or seeing his watch on the table, or seeing his papers and folders on the countertop. But back in May, after Mom played the entire album from the Moody Blues, she stood up, put all of Dad's things in boxes, and shoved them in our storage closet. I'd taken one of them back.

I tuned my radio—the one Dad and I had built—to 93.7 FM, and to guitar intros of the Moody Blues, I started making a list.

- a copy of a 1978 April issue of *Life* magazine

- brass cuff links

- an empty carton of Marlboros: Dad had quit when I turned ten.

- a Giants figurine

- a baseball cap

- pictures: Mom and Dad out for dinner with my grandparents, Laolao and Wai-Gong; Mom leaning on their rusted Chevy during their cross-country road trip honeymoon.

- a copy of the poem "When I Heard the Learn'd Astronomer" by Walt Whitman, with Mom's note scribbled on the bottom corner of the page: *I think you'd like this.*

- a roll of film

I looked at the picture of Mom and Dad on top of a mountain—in Yosemite, most likely—with Mom standing on a rock and her arms around Dad, her chin resting on his shoulder, and suddenly, I understood why Mom couldn't bear to look at these pictures anymore.

There was something stuck at the bottom of the box, and gently, I pulled it out.

A newspaper clipping from August 21, 1977.

VOYAGER LAUNCHES DESPITE SHAKY START, CARRYING EARTH'S SOUNDS TO THE COSMOS.

I remembered Dad sitting at the table with his steaming cup of coffee, carefully cutting it out from the newspaper.

"They've truly got everything in there," he'd said to Mom. "They've got pictures. They've got recordings of the human heartbeat and all sorts of cool stuff. Cheryl, this is history."

Mom sipped her tea. "Won't it get lost in all that space out there?"

"Exactly!" Dad said so excitedly that his scissors clattered to the table. "It's like sending a message in a bottle. We're putting a piece of ourselves out there so maybe someone—or something—could find it and see what we're all about. Imagine your picture being found a million years in the future. We get to be a part of outer space!"

"Come on, Richard," Mom said, but she smiled into her mug because she secretly liked it when Dad got all excited about things.

Over the next couple of days, Dad recorded every news segment that talked about the two *Voyager* space missions. "Look, Ro, they put whale songs on there too! And human greetings in sixty languages!"

Dad had dreamed about becoming an astronaut until the day his eyesight officially got too bad to allow it, but he still recorded every launch and space mission he could get his hands on.

I stared at all his things strewn around me, the trinkets and the papers and the pictures. I thought about today in my reading/LA class, when Mrs. Carey told us to bring in a thing that represented us. I thought about what I'd pick for Dad.

I couldn't let his things just sit in a box.

Then I suddenly got an idea.

I went over to my closet and opened the door, and reached for another box. I looked over the body of the rocket and the wires and nuts and bolts.

Dad and I had already gathered a few of our materials. He'd gotten me two rocket motors and planks of balsa wood for the fins. He'd even bought a nose cone. We'd already attached the airframe—the body of the rocket—to the nose cone. Dad and I had sketched out pages of designs. We'd calculated the dimensions of our rocket.

But that was it, really. We'd only scratched the surface, and now the actual work—setting up the payloads and the things that actually went inside the rocket and made it fly—were all up to me. And the more I scoured the *Handbook of Model Rocketry*, the more materials I realized were missing. I had to build the entire electric ignition—the thing that activated the motor and counted down the launch—by myself. Dad had planned to buy me a rocket camera from the Estes catalog to keep track of the flight, but I knew Mom and I could never afford that now.

Still, I couldn't stop staring at the half-built rocket some more, and then at the pile of Dad's things, and slowly, the curiously impossible idea sank in.

I'd always dreamed of building rockets someday, but it had never occurred to me that *I* could launch Dad's things into outer space. I could put his cuff links and the picture of him and Mom and his Giants figurine into a box, and the rocket could carry it past Mars and Jupiter and far, far into the galaxy. And in a million years, if someone or something found this rocket, floating through space like a message in a bottle, they'd open it up and see the cuff links and the picture of Dad smiling with his arms around Mom, their giddy smiles saved forever.

I just had to learn how to build a rocket first.

I reached for the folder and opened it up, forgetting that it wasn't mine. The paper was crinkled where the water had spilled. Still, the purple-folder boy was a good artist—really good, actually. There were aliens. A drawing of a planet that looked like Saturn, kind of, if Saturn were blue and purple. Comic explosions and speech bubbles and bright splashes of colors, mixed together. His pencil lines traced down in smooth curves that slowly became hard, straight angles.

I closed the folder.

I could try to get the rest of the supplies. I couldn't buy a rocket camera, but maybe I could build a radio transmitter instead. The parts weren't expensive. And I could make one from scratch—Dad and I had built radios before. I had money saved from Chinese New Year's and birthdays.

It was all *possible.*

I took out every single tool I had in the Rocket Box. I redrew my sketches for the rocket and did some calculations. I reached for my legal pad and flipped to a new sheet. On the top I wrote *List of Missing Materials* and underlined it.

The Next Best Step, I decided, was to finish building this rocket. After I got my notes back, of course.

CHAPTER FOUR
BENJI

OKAY, I HAD exactly three seconds to panic.

One Mississippi, two Mississippi, three—

It really *was* gone. I stared at the other folders. Math was the red folder. Reading/Language Arts, the yellow. Science, green. None of them had labels. But the purple folder, the one that I actually cared about—the one with my entire set of comics and the doodles of aliens and random three-dimensional cubes and whatever else I drew when I was bored—was missing, with another purple folder, neatly labeled *Science*, in its place.

I had no time. Danny was coming any minute now. I peered into the parking lot, but I didn't see his car. Maybe I had a minute. To go back and see if—

A honk jolted me back around. Danny rolled down the

window of his car and stuck his head out. "Benji!"

I made my way to the beat-up bright blue Ford, to the driver's side. "Hey, Danny," I said quickly. "Look, is there any way I could run and get something?"

A couple of moms behind us in the pickup line honked.

"No can do," my brother said. "I'm almost late for my shift. Come on, get in."

With a sigh, I tossed my backpack inside. I looked out the window as Danny hummed to the radio, his fingers drumming on the steering wheel. Of course he was wearing his varsity letterman jacket over his work uniform—he never took that thing off. He seemed to be having a good day. But then again, school wasn't really a problem for my brother. Nothing was.

Danny peered over at me at a stoplight. "First day? How was it?"

I looked down at my damp backpack.

Everything Goes Wrong for Unsuspecting Seventh Grader!! Can He Turn Things Around and Save the Day in Time?

"It was all right," I finally said.

"Any classes you like?"

I picked at the worn car seat. "Art. Although Mom might pull me out of it for extra study hall."

He smiled sympathetically. "Nah, she wouldn't actually. She never did it to me."

27

I stared out the window. She would have, if Danny'd had the sixth-grade report card that I had. But of course he hadn't. "Dunno. She seemed pretty serious about it the other day."

Mom had two full-time jobs: nurse and Worrying About Benji. She even said I gave her extra wrinkles.

Danny shrugged and went back to finger-drumming, switching over to whistling as we pulled into the Hogan's General Store parking lot, the car rattling the whole way. The car always seemed to be on the verge of falling apart, but Danny was real proud of it because he'd bought it off some senior on the baseball team for a cheap five hundred bucks, and he'd paid for it all by himself too.

Mom was always wondering why I tagged along to Danny's job. I could have just biked home. I mean, Mom was closer to Mr. Voltz, the Hogan's manager, than either Danny or I were. She was the on-call nurse who'd always taken care of his wife in the hospital back when she was sick. Mom always stayed on after her shifts to chat with her or bring her some treats. She'd been real protective of her. Nowadays, my mom still brings over the occasional lasagna to Mr. Voltz's place, just to check on how he's doing. He doesn't seem to particularly like a lot of people. He and his wife used to decorate their whole house with Christmas lights and hand out full-size candy bars at Halloween and host summer barbecues, but after his wife died, people said he got kind of weird.

But, still, Mr. Voltz liked Mom, which meant that he was pretty okay with Danny and me. And so when Danny got a job at Hogan's, Mr. Voltz let me sit next to him on the counter and, if I was super-duper careful and didn't crease anything when I put them back, he let me read the comics on the newsstands. He also gave me the occasional Werther's caramel.

Mr. Voltz nodded to Danny and sent him off to organize the appliance shelves on E7, which left just us at the counter. Mr. Voltz leaned back against the wall.

You know how some people have a *thing* or two you remember them by? Like with Mom, it was her purple nurse scrubs and her poufy mane of reddish curls. With Danny, his *thing* was the varsity letterman jacket. But with Mr. Voltz, it was his stare. Big caterpillar-like eyebrows perched on top of his glasses, framing cobalt-blue eyes. And his suspenders. I couldn't think of anyone else who wore suspenders.

"Had a good day?" he asked shortly.

"Yeah," I said, and he grunted and turned back to sorting coupons.

That's also what I liked about Mr. Voltz. He wasn't one of those grown-ups who needled you with questions.

I wandered past the frozen food aisle. The doorbell jingled as a couple of other people came in. Back when Danny and I were little and it was the middle of August and it got so hot and dry and still in Sacramento that our brains couldn't function, we'd bike over to Hogan's and stand in the frozen food aisle, our noses pressed to the glass as cold air trickled out. Now, I moved on to the comics section.

It *was* good that I'd come today, actually. Maybe I could find an extra copy of *Spacebound*. Of course, it wasn't as good as owning one and getting to read it as much as I wanted and not having to worry about crinkling the pages. But it would do. Worst-case scenario, I'd settle for some *Justice League*.

I pulled out the purple folder. *Ro Geraghty* was printed on the right-hand corner in neat letters. Maybe I'd accidentally stuffed my comics in her folder.

Nope. It was too light.

She didn't scribble. She didn't have random spots of color or accidental spaghetti stains or enough messy fingerprinted smudges to drive an FBI agent up the wall. There were no drawings of planets or characters from *Spacebound* or random alien faces.

There was just a bunch of numbers. And a list of what seemed like some weird household items in the corner of one page, like Popsicle sticks and a doorbell and D-cell batteries. There were neatly printed words and numbers paired with curves and scrawled drawings with arrows pointing everywhere and weird cursive letters that had to mean some complicated math thing. That much I knew, even after getting almost a D last year in math. *Angle. Lift. Velocity.*

Huh.

It looked like hieroglyphics.

Maybe she'd taken my folder with her. Maybe she'd carried it home with her school stuff. Or maybe it was sitting forgotten on Toothpick's desk. Or maybe it was sitting in the lost and found, with all those gross gym socks and lost lunch bags with moldy bananas.

I turned back to the shelf, scouring for *Spacebound*.

I really, really hoped it wasn't sitting in the lost and found. It was gross to think of my drawings with the smell of dirty feet and rotting moldy banana all over—

I shut the folder and leaned back with a sigh.

Tomorrow's science class couldn't come fast enough.

Switching the folders back took about thirty seconds.

And then we didn't say a word to each other for the rest of class.

It wasn't that I didn't talk, really. It was just that out of all the people in Sacramento, I couldn't talk to most of them without my palms feeling itchy and my voice coming out too soft. And then they would ask, "What's that?" and then I would have to repeat the whole thing again. And whenever a teacher would say, "Let's do a couple of icebreakers," I'd start to sweat, because I really was fine if the ice didn't break, not even a little bit. Honestly, I would rather go to the dentist than speak up in class.

There wasn't much to say in class at this point, either. Toothpick was going on and on about some science-fair thing that he seemed to be way too excited about. "Be *creative*," he said, waving his arms around. "Students in the past years have done everything from looking at the growth of plants to measuring the amount of energy in Gatorade. No papier-mâché volcanoes allowed in here, all right?" He winked at us. "This is the big project that we'll be working on until March. You'll be working on it with one partner in this class. And who knows? Some teams in the past who have gone above and beyond have submitted their projects to the regional science fair in March for *major* extra credit points in this class." He wiggled his fingers when he said *extra credit*, like it would mean anything to us.

I went back to tuning him out. Even though I probably needed that extra credit real bad. Mom had been threatening to switch out my art class with extra study hall tutoring for a while now. But right now, I kind of just wanted to keep to myself and my sketchbook.

I mean, I was totally fine talking with some people. Like Amir. And Mom, even if most of the time it was just us arguing about when I would clean my room. And Danny, once in a while, when he wasn't away at a baseball game or at parties or at his friend's house or hogging our family phone line and calling his girlfriend, Chelsea. Or Drew, back before the Prank Wars. Or Mr. Keanan, the art teacher. He had hairy arms and a wild mop of hair and refused to wear a tie. He played the radio while we worked in class, threatened to throw a block of wet clay at Drew's head if he ever tried to pull something in his class, and let me eat lunch in the art room without having to say anything. He played the radio, and I drew and listened to the scratchy sound of my pencil against the paper. Mr. Keanan understood that it was way easier to think in color than in words. Like how it was easier to listen than talk. Plus, he'd started playing *The Hitchhiker's Guide to the Galaxy* on the radio, and not gonna lie, I was really starting to get into the plot.

But man, I missed Amir. He was the only person I could really talk to about comics. Or about my dad. Or both. If I had to point to the start of the search for my dad, really, it probably was the day I got to know Amir. Also known as the day of the chicken-wing incident.

Or maybe it was the day I found the drawing. But that came later.

I became friends with Amir Karimi in our sixth-grade science class when he fainted while slicing open raw chicken wings.

The teacher hadn't told us about the dissection until the week before. I didn't know what "die-section" was, really, until someone raised their hand and Mr. Martin explained that, yes, this "die-section" thing did involve raw chicken wings but that no, there wasn't supposed to be blood and guts everywhere because the chicken wings would be cleaned. But I didn't hear most of this because I'd been doodling plants and vines in the corner of my notebook.

"Okay, everybody, partner up."

I snuck glances at Drew goofing off with his new friend Eddie in the corner of the room. I thought we'd be friends again—it had been two weeks since the Prank Wars had ended—but he hadn't said a word to me, and the sight of him making fun of the teacher with that trademark smile of his made me sick. It was kind of weird to be replaced, to be honest. But at that moment, I realized that it would actually be kind of okay if he never talked to me again.

Which meant that on the morning of the dissection, I was paired with Amir, a small, skinny kid who'd looked shaky at the sight of a tiny, rubber-like chicken wing. He flinched when I prodded the wing with a small scalpel, and when it was his turn to handle the tools, he accidentally hit a vein in the chicken wing and promptly collapsed on my shoulder.

While the class flipped out about someone fainting, I practically carried him to the nurse's office. Amir woke up twenty minutes later, and we got to skip all of science class.

After that incident, we started sitting together at lunch every day. I learned that Amir lived with his parents and three sisters but had to leave behind his grandparents and friends when he left Iran. When I was still friends with Drew he'd make fun of Amir's accent, but I learned that Amir was one of the smartest people I'd ever met and was fluent in Farsi and English and a little bit of French, and only said the word *garage* funny because he'd lived in England for a year before moving here. I learned that Amir's maman and baba had both taught in a city called Tehran, until the government changed and got scary and they had to move away. I told Amir about how my mom was hardly ever home because she worked twelve-hour shifts at the hospital and how my dad was *really* never home because, well, he and my mom divorced a long time ago and I hadn't seen him since I was four. I told him about how my mom stress-cleaned the house and always called home between work shifts to make sure I was doing okay, and how every teacher I'd ever had had told me how much they loved my brother.

Sure, there were some differences between us. Amir's favorite American candy was Good & Plenty; I liked Red Vines. He separated his foods when he ate because he couldn't stand them mixed together; I loved combining things like pretzels and grape jelly to see what it was like. If I were to draw Amir, there wouldn't be a line out of place; his green checkered shirt collars were always neatly folded down, his hair combed, his pants the right length. He was always making fun of how my brother's hand-me-down baseball-tournament shirts were too big on me. But other than all that, I swear, sometimes I thought we were the same person. And the best part? He read comics too. I didn't have to explain why I loved them so much, like I'd had to explain to Drew.

See, the thing was, life was a lot more exciting with the possibility of getting superpowers someday and getting sent on some epic mission to save the world. Or, at least, school became a lot more bearable.

Amir and I caught up on all the latest issues of *The Flash* and *Batman*. He mostly read his comics when he came over to my house, though, because his maman said that comics were a waste of time. One of those times, when I was looking for extra sketchbooks that Mom had stored in some bins in the garage, I found a drawing that'd gotten stuck to one of the covers.

"Whoa," I said. "Dude, look at this."

I thought it was a page that had accidentally been torn out of some comic book at first, but I took another look and saw splotches of water stains on the page and blurred colored-pencil lines.

It was definitely an original work of art. But I couldn't tell which comic it was from, which was weird.

Amir peered over.

"Oh, I didn't know you liked *Spacebound*," he said.

"What?"

"That." Amir pointed to the drawing. "You drew that really well. It looks *exactly* like *Spacebound*."

"But I didn't draw it," I said. I barely made out the name scrawled in the corner. *David Allen Burns.*

"Wait," I said. "That's my dad." I hadn't seen his name in so long that I almost didn't recognize it. Truth be told, I knew less about my dad than I knew about my neighbor Mrs. Simmons. At least I knew what she looked like. And that she had three mean cats.

Amir cocked an eyebrow. "Your dad drew . . . *this*?"

I shrugged. "Probably. Looks like it."

He stared at me like I was telling him the earth was flat or something.

"Then . . . you've read his comics, right?"

I turned around in disbelief. "He writes comics?"

And that was how I found out my dad wrote *Spacebound*.

I was captivated by the comics from volume 1, issue 1. Maybe it was the story about Captain Gemma Harris, whose space crew accidentally ended up on a dusty planet billions of light-years from Earth after one of the radioactive experiments on their ship went horribly wrong. Maybe it was the characters they met in the alternate universes on their journey home—from bands of evil three-eyed aliens intent on finding and conquering Earth, to the Bardlebums, a troupe who traveled from universe to universe with wacky musical performances titled (wait for it) Space Operas, to Woz, the adorable abandoned spacepup that Gemma adopted.

Or maybe it was the wacky jokes my dad made, or the way the artwork matched up exactly with the drawings I'd dug up from the depths of the storage bin.

The point was:

I was hooked on these comics.

and

I knew now that my dad was out there. Somewhere.

And in volume 3, issue 2, *Mission Unearthed*, when

Captain Gemma Harris found out that her dad wasn't dead but missing somewhere in the universe, she went on a mission to track him down.

I swear, the hair on my neck stood up.

"Do you think I could maybe"—I cleared my throat over my peanut butter sandwich—"you know, find him?"

Amir wiped his hands on a napkin. "Sure. You got his address?"

"I mean, no."

"Phone number?"

"Not really."

"I don't know, then. He could live in New York, for all we know. Or maybe even Iowa."

He scooped some rice out of his thermos. "I read in a book that there are more cows in Iowa than people. How would you find him in a sea of cows?"

After school at Hogan's the next week, I was in the middle of re-creating a *Spacebound* drawing of Captain Gemma Harris in her space suit when I saw a familiar flash of blue and white.

Wait a second.

I peeked over the edge of the aisle.

It was her. Ro Geraghty. The girl from my science class, with her baggy blue-and-white windbreaker and her hair half pulled up in a white hair tie, standing alone in line until Danny waved to her. She marched right up to the counter, her arms full. In the mound of objects she dumped in front of my brother, I saw scissors, a packet of paper clips, electrical tape, a bunch of glue bottles, Popsicle sticks, and nuts and bolts.

As Danny rang her up, I realized that those were all things on that list I'd seen. The list in her purple folder, along with pages of all those mysterious numbers.

Seriously, what on *earth* was she up to?

Maybe this was some kind of arts-and-crafts project. I knew almost for sure it was related to the thing she kept scribbling on about in her secret notebook during science class. She did exactly what I did: she placed her secret notebook inside her green science notebook to pretend like she was taking notes.

I caught glimpses of her secret notebook sometimes. I mean, I hadn't meant to, and I knew it was kind of wrong to snoop on other people's business. But I was curious, and I thought that maybe if I stared long enough the hieroglyphics would start to morph and make sense or something. Plus, she had to have looked inside my folder a little bit. I'd caught her peeking at my drawings a couple of times, but every time I glanced up, she looked away. I gotta say, we nailed this not-talking thing.

Maybe it was a top-secret project.

A top-secret government project.

Spy Prodigy Infiltrates Middle School to Save It from a Lurking Danger! Can She—

"Do you have any D-cell batteries?"

I was getting carried away with this.

Danny said, "Nah, I don't think so. We have double-A, or the smaller triple-As?"

"It's way bigger. I guess a 12-volt could work, too, but I thought D-cell batteries would be easier to find."

What *was* she working on?

"Huh," Danny said, leaning on the counter. "Haven't seen those around here. I can ask my manager, but he's taking a break right now."

That was true. Mr. Voltz usually sat at his normal spot against the counter, with his back flat against the wall, but he'd gone out to get something from his car a while ago.

The fan whirred behind me. I put my pencil down. I could swear that when I was walking down the aisle today . . .

"Well," she said, "I'll try somewhere else, I guess."

Danny handed her the receipt.

Bingo.

I had seen those big, bulky batteries in aisle E6. I knew because it was right across from the comic books and magazines.

Ro was about to leave. Before I knew it, I was running after her. The bell clanged as the door closed behind me.

"E6," I blurted out.

Ro turned around, her eyes wide.

"That's where it is. The thing. I mean, the battery. The

battery thing you were looking for. Danny just missed it."

She raised an eyebrow. "Danny?"

"Oh, yeah. My brother." *Not helpful, Benji.* "The cashier back there." I cleared my throat. "The battery is in aisle E6, though. I promise."

She smiled. She had a nice smile, actually, when she didn't have that kinda-spacey-kinda-freaked-out expression she'd had all of last week. "Thanks."

This is what I should have done: smiled back and said "You're welcome" like a regular normal person.

This is what I actually did: I blurted out, "Are you building a radio?"

I, apparently, was not a regular normal person.

She tilted her head. "What?"

"I mean, what you're working on. Is it a radio or something?"

"Why would you think that?"

I looked down at my shoes, my palms beginning to itch. At that moment, I really wished I were the Flash. Don my suit, and *boom.* I'd be outta there.

"No—sorry, I didn't mean it like that," she said. "I know you looked at my drawings." She wasn't even mad about it. She just said it, matter-of-fact. Maybe with even a little bit of a smile. "I was just wondering what made you think it was a radio."

"I mean, it was my best guess. I couldn't really tell." Those Popsicle sticks really threw me for a loop.

41

She set her stuff down. "Guesses like?"

I shrugged. "Robot, maybe. Clock. Time machine."

I'd tossed the last one out there mostly as a joke because I'd seen those sci-fi movies have time machines made out of radioactive boxes, but her eyes widened. "You think I'm building a time machine?"

"I was just—"

"I mean, could that be scientifically possible, do you think? Like a box that could travel space and time? Like—"

"The TARDIS," I said. Amir loved that show.

"Exactly!" she said. "From *Doctor Who*."

Our eyes met. I smiled, just a little bit.

"So, am I right?"

"You're in the ballpark," she said, straightening up.

"What, you're actually building a time-traveling space machine?"

"Minus the time-traveling part."

"A spaceship?"

She raised her eyebrow.

I stared at her. "You're actually—"

"A rocket," she said with a grin, "to be exact." She looked past me, toward the store. "Wanna show me where this battery is?"

"Get brainstorming with your partners," Toothpick said. He was on his second cup of coffee, so he was pacing around the tables, gesturing wildly with his hands as he announced that *today* was the day to get excited about, because we were building Rube Goldberg machines, those things that launched a ball from a cup to a lever to a chute, bouncing it from one contraption to another until it finally rang a bell or dropped into a bucket. "The best one gets a week of no homework."

People around us squealed and turned to their partners. Ro ripped a sheet of paper out of her notebook and turned to me. She rolled up the sleeves of her windbreaker. There was already a full sketch. "Here. It should work, as long as the bottom doesn't collapse."

Of course she was already a million steps ahead. I got to work.

Around us, everyone was talking, but Ro and I didn't say another word to each other.

Maybe I should have said something. I mean, we'd practically had a whole conversation a few days ago. But then I thought about my throat getting all funny and my face getting hot. It's like those moments when you're in an elevator with someone, or when you're sitting next to someone in the nurse's office. And you make eye contact and you know that you're supposed to say something so your mom doesn't say you're being rude, even if it's something dumb like what the weather is. But then too much time has passed, and it's harder and harder to start a conversation, and so you sit in silence and stare at the wall or wait for the elevator to ding.

As I pushed aside my drawings to make more space, Ro

asked, "What's that all about?"

I looked up. "I'm building the base like you said."

"No, that." Ro looked at my drawings. "I've been trying to figure that out for weeks."

She was looking directly at my hastily scribbled map, the starred cities, and a rough drawing of my dad. Instinctively, I pulled the drawings back.

"Who *is* that?"

My mouth went dry. *No one*, I wanted to say, but it came out as, "My dad."

"Is he traveling or something?"

I shrugged, hoping she'd drop it. "Something like that. I don't really know."

She put down the two blocks she was taping together. "What do you mean, you don't know?"

"I don't," I said. It came out kind of sharp, and I could tell she was hurt, because she looked down and turned away a little.

I felt bad. She'd told me what she was working on, so I felt like she at least should get something. "I don't really know. He's not with us anymore."

Ro looked up with wide eyes.

"No!" I felt my face turning red. "Not like that. He's not like, dead or anything." I added a lever to the bottom of the bucket. "He's just . . . not around in my family anymore." I could feel my face turning redder.

"Oh." Ro slumped back into her seat. She gave me a

look, but it wasn't that scrunched-up pitying look that parents and teachers always gave me when they found out that my parents were divorced. And it wasn't one of those functional divorces, like how Holly Berger's parents bought houses on opposite sides of Sacramento and divided her weekends equally between them. But Ro didn't look like she felt sorry for me. She looked like she was trying to figure something out. "So you don't talk to him?"

I shrugged. "I don't know his number. Or where he is. I just read his stuff." I nodded at the comics.

Ro picked up the comics. "He wrote these? Your dad?"

"Pretty sure he did, yeah." I paused. "Did you . . . read it?"

"Oh, when we switched on accident?" She closed the cover of the comic. "Nope. But the cover looks cool."

I breathed a sigh of relief.

"He doesn't write these anymore?"

"Still does," I said. "They come out every four months." I clicked the last part of the Rube Goldberg machine into place and set the marble at the top to roll down.

"So," Ro said.

She met my eyes, and I swear, I could *see* the gears practically *click-click-clicking* in her mind.

"So he's still out there writing these comics?"

"Maybe," I said, as if I didn't care. As if I hadn't rooted through our entire house when Mom wasn't looking, as if I hadn't torn through the filing cabinets in case there was another drawing that he could have left behind. As if

45

I didn't count down the days until each *Spacebound* issue came out in the grocery store.

"I've tried reaching out to him before. He never answered." The marble clattered down. I stared at the machine. The marble wasn't fitting through one of the bridges. I held up one of the pieces. "It's fitted wrong."

Ro frowned at her drawing. "But I thought—"

"It doesn't entirely fit in," I said. "When the marble passes through it'll collapse. We could try this." I clicked it into place. The marble slid through perfectly.

She didn't say anything for a second. I glanced up and she was giving me a look. "What?"

"Nothing." A slow grin spread. "Nice job."

Out of the corner of my eye, I saw Drew in the back corner of the classroom with his partner, Eddie, telling someone to come look and see if his machine was functioning.

When Jimmy approached and leaned down to inspect it—*splat*—a hidden spoon catapult sprang up, flinging Jell-O onto his face.

"Sorry!" Drew said. "Guess I got a bit of my lunch stuck in there."

Everyone around the table roared with laughter. Jimmy peeled the strawberry Jell-O off his face and smiled real hard, but his cheeks were bright. I looked away and felt a little awful.

Ro didn't laugh. She glanced over and scowled, which made me feel slightly better. She turned back. "This is why you drew that map, isn't it? You're trying to find him."

I dropped the marble from the top, not meeting her eyes. She didn't even need a guessing game. She got it right on the first try.

"Hey, I told you about my rocket."

She was right. I looked her square in the eye. "Yeah, I am. Or I was. Pretty dumb, right?" The marble clattered perfectly down each of the steps, and then through the tunnel that I'd built, and then down the chute I put to replace Ro's tunnel. It dropped into the bucket. The lever launched it through to another tunnel, where it clattered through to the final chute. It hit the bell and dinged.

I looked up. "We did it!"

When the bell rang, I grabbed back the drawings and the comics, tucked them into my folder, and then made sure that they were both safely in my backpack.

"Hey," she said, before I turned to leave. She nodded at the drawings. "You're really good at this, you know."

I grinned. "Thanks."

Come to think of it, this wasn't the worst lab partner setup in the world. Plus, we were actually kind of great at working together. We even had a normal conversation today—well, except for the part where I told her I was trying to find my long-lost dad through a trail of his comics. But still, she didn't seem weirded out at all. Which was a good sign.

Things were looking up.

CHAPTER FIVE
RO

SCIENTISTS LIKE UNCOVERING secrets. They'll go into deep jungles filled with snakes and flesh-eating ants just to find a new plant species. They can brush off a single shell and use it to figure out how old the earth is. They want to figure out everything—how fast a hummingbird flies, how mountains expand and shrink in hot and cold weather, how our skin learns to heal itself after we accidentally slip and get rug burn.

Dad was a chemist, which meant that he mixed together acids in a lab until they sizzled and made something new. At home, he figured out the exact ratio of blue and purple food coloring to use to make the perfect periwinkle frosting for Mom's birthday cake. When we went to Disneyland, Dad stayed behind to watch a magic show, watching the man flip cards over and over again, eyes trained on the man's white-gloved hands until he had figured out the trick, then ran after us to explain it. And when we were driving back from the supermarket one night and there was a flash of orange in the sky, Dad turned off the radio and pulled over to the side of the road, and in the still silence we looked up at the night sky and wondered what had happened.

I got Dad's science genes. Or so Mom has told me ever since she saw me measuring milk to get the perfect Cocoa-Puffs-to-milk balance. When I first heard the word *genes*, I thought of the pants you wear, and so for months I went around thinking that if you wore their jeans, you could be good at certain things. Like if I wore Mom's high-waisted jeans, I could speed through novels in an hour and visit the Crocker Art Museum without getting bored. Instead, I got Dad's worn Levi's genes, and that meant that I figured out secrets in millimeters and *tick-tick-tick*s of a clock. It meant that I understood numbers better than I could figure out what kids were saying when they whispered about me. It meant that when I came across a newspaper article about a Russian satellite that had burned up in the atmosphere and caused an orange flash, I rushed to Dad to show him. It meant that every once in a while when we were driving that same road back from the supermarket, I would ask Dad to pull over. We'd open the trunk and sit at the back with our blankets, and we'd search the night sky because space was full of things to figure out: the distance between stars, the path of a comet, what it would be like to step on Mars.

I liked uncovering secrets, and here it was. A big, fat, juicy secret from Benji.

I couldn't stop thinking about it as I sorted Dad's stuff. I put trinkets in one pile. Papers and pictures in another.

Benji's dad was somewhere out there. He still published comics that came out every four months.

The question was—

Where *was* he?

It was like one of those big puzzle projects, the kind with a thousand pieces where I wouldn't know where to start. But I'd figure out the corner pieces. And the edges. And I'd work faster and faster, until the puzzle finally started to come together.

I just had to figure out the corner pieces. A phone number. A publisher's address.

I carefully took out another picture. It was Mom and Dad, sitting in Mission Dolores Park, with the buildings of San Francisco rising in the distance. Mom had pink-framed sunglasses. Dad wore a big striped shirt and had his arm around Mom, his hair a wild, unruly mess. Nana once told me that Dad had had a hippie phase; his hair was longer than Mom's at one point. In the picture, Mom was laughing into Dad's shoulder.

It was never a mystery how Dad died. In fact, I've known how it happened ever since the night the cop showed up at our door. How it occurred between ten p.m. and eleven p.m. How it happened on that same winding road to Ral-ey's. How the alcohol that made up exactly .25 percent of the other driver's bloodstream was more than enough to cause him to veer onto the other side of the road at a velocity of seventy miles per hour, at an angle that led him directly to where Dad was.

I knew what all the details were, but this time the details weren't enough for me. It didn't explain why an average person lived to be sixty-seven years old and Dad didn't get twenty-two of them. The police never told me how to finish sixth grade or spend a summer with a black hole growing in my chest.

I set the picture of Mom and Dad down and leaned against the wall.

My dad was never coming back. That much I knew.

But Benji's dad could.

I couldn't sit still. And after a moment, I reached for my notepad and started a new list.

CHAPTER SIX
BENJI

"WE'RE FINDING HIM."

Ro plopped something between us, breaking the unofficial Science Table Divide.

I looked up from the latest *X-Men* issue. "Huh?"

The letters were printed perfectly on the sheet of paper she'd dropped on the table: *Reuniting Benjamin Burns with His Long-Lost Father.*

"Like I said"—she leaned in—"we're finding your dad."

I stammered, "We?"

"Yeah, I'm helping you." She grinned.

Whoa, *what*?

I peered at the paper. She hadn't actually written anything else down, but there were ten bullet points, spaced exactly the same width apart. She'd even written this list on graph paper. *Graph paper.*

She was actually such a nerd.

Ro said, "What do you say?"

"I mean, I wasn't even that serious about finding him," I lied. "It's just wishful thinking, really. It's not like some Indiana Jones mystery. He's impossible to find, Ro. Really. He didn't leave behind an address or a phone number or *anything*."

"So? We can still put together some kind of plan. We have his comic books." She leaned in some more. "We have two brains. A map."

"And way too many number-two pencils."

"Huh?"

"Never mind." I frowned. "What makes you want to do this so badly?"

She shrugged. "I just like figuring things out."

Suddenly an idea came to me. I cleared my throat. "Okay, yeah, you can help. But one thing, though."

She tilted her head.

"If you're helping me with this," I said slowly, then swallowed, "I'm helping you build your rocket."

She raised her eyebrows.

"You really don't have to," she said quickly. "You don't have to do something for me just because I'm doing something for—"

"Can't hurt to have help."

She pushed up her sleeves even more. "Technically it can. If the measurements are not calibrated right or if the design's even a bit off—"

"Okay." I sighed. "I'll stay out of your way with the building stuff and the cali-whatever. Just let me do whatever helps you. And, you know, we could even put it in the science fair."

She peered at me suspiciously. "You're either asleep or drawing half the time in class. Since when do you care about the science fair?"

Turns out, when your mom is threatening to take away the only class you actually care about, you can care about it a whole lot.

"Hey, I really need the extra credit. My mom says if I don't do well in science then she'll switch out art class with extra study hall. But I'll be helpful, I promise."

Ro raised her eyebrows and then shrugged. "Okay, fine." She straightened up. "Fine. You can help me with my rocket."

I reached up to the sheet, crossed off my name, and changed it to *Benji*. "And you can help me find my dad."

Ro grinned wide, the kind where the corners of her eyes crinkled and I could see the freckles on her cheeks real clear. It was the kind of beaming grin that somehow made *me* kind of excited, too. "Deal." She reached out her hand.

"We gotta spit on it," I said, with a completely serious face.

She pulled it back. "Gross! You know how many germs are in saliva? I would never—"

"Kidding," I said, with a grin. "Gotcha."

We shook hands.

"First," I said, shoving a pile of *Spacebound* comics over to her, "you've got some reading to do."

CHAPTER SEVEN
RO

I HURRIED INTO science class the next day and set the stack of *Spacebound* comics down on our table.

Benji raised an eyebrow. "Whatcha think?"

"You got the next issue?"

A slow smile crept over his expression. "You loved it."

I composed myself. "It was all right. A little imaginative, sometimes. Some parts of it are a little unrealistic. Like, a human can't actually survive being pulled through a black hole because the energy would crush them. And galaxies take light-years to merge, not two weeks. But—"

"Oh, *come on*," Benji said, not believing me for a second. "I gave you six issues and you read them all in a day. You loved it."

"Okay, I did!" I picked up the comics and hugged them to my chest, unable to contain my grin. I'd stayed up past midnight last night, something I never did because it would mess up my circadian rhythms. "How could I not? There's a *spacepup*. And do we find out if she escapes from those three-eyed aliens? Or if she discovers more of her super-powers with the Titanium Rod?"

"I can't spoil anything," Benji said with a wicked grin. He pushed over another copy. "But here's the next one."

I set the comics back down and cleared my throat. "Okay, speaking of these, we should really focus on—"

I was cut short by the bell. Mr. Devlin walked in, wearing a tie full of smiley faces.

"Okay, folks. Get excited, because today we're talking about acids and bases." He set his coffee mug down and leaned over his lab table.

I turned around. Benji opened his notebook and started doodling a planet, rings and all. I waited for a moment to speak, because I had it all planned out in my head, but Mr. Devlin kept talking, all while drawing huge molecules on the board and talking about how acids stole electrons from bases like pickpockets.

I couldn't wait until the end of class.

I reached for the edge of my notebook, where I knew Benji would see. I printed out, *So let's get this started.*

Benji stopped sketching his rings.

He scrawled, under my writing, *Get what started?*

I smiled to myself. I wrote, *Finding your long-lost father, of course.*

Benji: *Oh, you're actually serious about this thing.*

I'm always serious.

Benji looked up. *Okay, Captain.*

I wrote, *Meet after school today?*

He paused, and then scribbled, *My house. I've got some more comics back there.*

Me: *Possibly volume 2, issue 7?*

Him: *Patience.*

"You have to be careful with some acids," Mr. Devlin went on. "Some of them are highly corrosive. They can dissolve metal or, at times, human flesh."

The class went, "Ewwwwww."

I tuned back into class and started taking notes.

Benji kept on sketching. I leaned over and wrote in the corner of my notebook, *Stop drawing and pay attention, doofus.*

He saw my writing and laughed a little bit, and then turned my Os into a set of monster eyes. He then drew a wave of acid eating up the monster's arm. With a few pencil marks, he'd turned the monster's expression into a look of horror.

Who says I wasn't?

I stared at the wave of drawings taking over my neatly printed numbers and my carefully hand-drawn periodic table, but I couldn't help but smile to myself. He was hopeless. I turned back to Mr. Devlin.

As I biked to Benji's house after school, with him doing small pop wheelies off the sides of the curbs, I realized that

Benji lived only five blocks away from me, on Chestnut Avenue. How had our paths never crossed?

I guess I just never knew any of the kids near me who went to the public school. I'd never really met Drew Balonik, the kid a street over who set off the fireworks this summer, but now I saw him everywhere, usually with his friends, or friendly-teasing Charlotte.

"You nerd," Benji said over his shoulder. "You really brought a clipboard and everything?"

"Told you I was serious about this."

"You know, I just realized. Mom's probably going to be mad that I invited someone over without cleaning up."

"What do you mean?" I looked around. Some things stood out. Like the bright orange pillows on the blue couch, or the ratty braided rug or floral curtains. But the books on the shelves were sorted, the dish towels stacked neatly on top of each other. In my kitchen, my mom wasn't afraid of a mess, often dusting flour down the entire counter and even the floor a little when she made cookies, or accidentally leaving out a pot of soup when she was running late for her open houses. I made a note to myself to color-code our books, too.

"Oh, not here," he said. "I was talking about my room. Hold on, I just have to get some things."

Benji's room was an entirely different story. The walls were painted dark blue. Things were piled all over the floor. Old sketchbooks and school folders lay haphazardly on top of each other. A set of broken chalk lay strewn on a news-paper. A beat-up skateboard in the corner. I stood in the doorway, in the small patch of carpet that wasn't covered by comics or sketches or stray socks.

"Trust me," he said, catching my look of doubt. "I know where everything is, I swear." He poked around a stack of comics, pulling a couple out. He then rooted under the bed and pulled out a whole carton of Red Vines.

"You hide snacks under your bed?"

"My mom doesn't like me eating them," he said. "She's a nurse, so she's strict about that kinda stuff. She says there's some kind of preservatives or red dye in there that's bad for me. It's like she thinks I'll grow an extra arm or some-thing."

I caught a glimpse of even more cartons under his bed.

"It's like what the Boy Scouts say." He handed the car-ton to me. "Be prepared and all that."

There were enough Red Vines packets stashed to last a nuclear winter. He reached down and pulled out a can of Pepsi. He cracked it open and took a long swig, to my incredulous look. "I'm not a nurse," I said, "but that has got to be a little too much sugar."

"No such thing," he said. "Plus, we're going on an epic detective mission. Gotta fuel up." He bounded up to me. "Ready?"

We spread out the comics on his living room coffee table and sat down, our backs against the worn couch. I bit the end off a Red Vine. "Okay, let's do this. First we're going to reach out to Arcade Comics—"

"Already did," Benji said. "I wrote two letters to them. Even called them once. No one answered their phone. And they didn't respond to my letters."

"What about asking your mom about him?"

"She won't talk about him," Benji said flatly. "She gets kinda mad every time I bring him up. I've found, like, maybe two pictures of him around the house, but otherwise it's like he was never here."

I crossed out my first two bullet points. *Okay, then.*

I looked up at the shelf above the TV, which was crammed with medals. "I didn't know you play baseball."

"I don't." Benji shrugged. "Well, I did, but it's mostly my brother now. He's real good."

"Oh." I glanced at the pictures in front of the trophy. Come to think of it, his brother did look a lot like Benji. They had the same mop of dirty-blond curls and smile. "So he's at practice right now? I thought he worked at the store."

"For now," he said. "He works during his off-season."

"You work there too?"

Benji smiled. "Nope. Mr. Voltz lets me hang around and read comics."

"He's my neighbor, actually," I said. "We don't talk much, though." But enough about that—we had to focus. "Okay," I said. I drew a big circle around Sacramento and then starred it. "This is where he was." With a pencil, I drew arrows pointing out. "And now, he's somewhere else."

"He could even be out of the country. What if he's in Greenland? Or Iceland? Or whichever one has the snow on it. I always get them mixed up."

"Probably not," I said doubtfully. "He's a comic book artist, not a wanted fugitive."

"Okay, you're right." He bit the end off a Red Vine. "So, let's say he's in the country. Where do we start?"

"From the beginning," I said. I flipped to the cover of volume 1, issue 1. "So this first came out three years ago. November 1980, to be exact. Was he still here then?"

Benji shook his head. "He left when I was, like, four. Way before these comics came out."

I quickly did the math. Benji and I were the same age, and so he must have left around eight years ago. Five years before he wrote *Spacebound*. "And you're certain David Allen is your dad."

Benji smoothed out a piece of paper in front of me. "I think it's a pen name. His full name's David Allen Burns. And besides, look. This was lying around our house. The drawings match up to those comics."

The letters on the sheet were rounded and bubbly, whereas the ones on the published comic had sharper edges. But the color scheme—red and blue and this specific shade of mustard yellow that was a little too bright—was all there. And unmistakably, Gemma Harris—with her cape and her steel-tipped boots—was there, too, sailing into midair.

It was signed in the bottom corner: *David Allen Burns*.

A shiver ran through me.

"Yeah," I said softly. "This is definitely him."

I looked up. "You're *positive* he doesn't have a phone number or anything."

Benji shook his head and picked at the corner of the couch, where one of the seams had split. "The last phone number that Mom had for him in our house's address book doesn't work anymore."

I peered at the number. It was an 818 area code, which came from . . .

I reached for a YellowPages phone book and skimmed through it. "Pasadena," I said. I searched the map. It was a town just north of Los Angeles. I went back to the phone book. Nothing.

No address, no phone number. Benji had already told me that, but I thought with a little poking around, we could find *something*.

"Okay," I said, trying to think. I flipped through the issues.

Benji peered at me. "Are you sure you want to do this? I mean, I totally get it if you don't. It could be a total waste of time. My friend Amir once said that some states like Iowa have more cows than people, so it would be like trying to find someone in a sea of cows. Or a needle in a haystack. I guess the second one makes more sense."

"First of all," I said, "Iowa isn't *full* of cows. My dad's parents are from there. Also, we made a deal, remember? I'm helping you find him." I looked up at him, and my throat felt tight all of a sudden. I said softly, "Think of how cool it would be if you saw him again."

Benji looked down. He was quiet for a moment. "You're right. Besides, I think he *wants* me to find him."

I set the comics down. "What do you mean?"

"Okay, well, I know you haven't read to this point so I'm probably spoiling this for you, but—"

"Doesn't matter." Maybe it mattered a *little* bit, but still, we had to find his dad. "Tell me."

"So, volume 3, issue 2," he said, laying it out in front of me. "It came out maybe six months ago. Gemma Harris discovers that her dad has been held captive on an exoplanet all along."

I sat up. "You mean she isn't an orphan like she thought?"

Benji shook his head. "Nope. Turns out, her dad was a space traveler before her, but he got stuck in another galaxy and he's been trying to find his way back to Earth since. So she has to go on a mission to find him."

Captain Gemma Harris has to go find her dad.

Just like—

Our eyes met.

"You see?" Benji said, almost whispering. "It's almost like he's sending me a message."

"Like he wants you to *find him*," I said.

64

"Yeah."

It wasn't just a big secret anymore. It wasn't just a mystery that you could look at and think about from time to time.

It was a mission.

A bona fide *mission*.

My heart started racing. It wasn't just us trying to find his dad. His dad wanted us to find him. "That means the clues *have* to be in the comics!" I reached for the comics excitedly. An idea sprang to my mind. "Maybe . . . we can just look in the first couple of issues, where . . ."

"Where it's still set on Earth!" Benji said.

I skimmed the first pages. "So, mountains, deserts, some town," I said. "She's in a secret government science lab." I looked up. "Maybe he's in the Southwest somewhere. Like Arizona or New Mexico." I flipped through to the next couple of pages. "But then she gets brought to Washington, DC."

Aha. Our first official city name. I wrote it down on my clipboard.

I pushed away the atlas and the phone book, and spread out the comics, and circled every Earth location I could find in *Spacebound*.

We were getting somewhere. The puzzle pieces were beginning to come together, and I got that excited feeling again, the tingle in my gut, the feeling when I didn't quite know how it would all unfold, but I could see that it was the beginning of *something*.

CHAPTER EIGHT
BENJI

RO LIVED EXACTLY a block away from Drew Balonik, which meant that a) I knew the exact way to her house, and b) the entire time we were biking over there after school, I was sincerely hoping I wouldn't run into him.

When Ro and I came in, her mom was chatting away on the phone, waving her hands around, but when she saw us, her eyes lit up and she waved and mouthed, *Hi!*

"Client call, probably," Ro whispered to me. "She's a real estate agent. We can just—"

"Hi, honey!" Ro's mom rushed around to the kitchen table. "And you must be Benji!" She reached out for a hug, smiling, and then held me at arm's length. "Ro has told me all about you."

Ro's mom reminded me of those energetic people who worked out on TV in neon leotards and made burpees look a lot more fun than they actually were, except she was dressed up in fancy clothes and wore lipstick. She kind of looked like Ro, actually, just with straight jet-black hair and bangs. And a lot of makeup. If I were to draw Ro's mom, I wouldn't use colored pencils; I would use those bright markers Mr. Keanan had.

"Are you hungry, Benji?" She opened the fridge and started rooting around. "We've got some snacks we could heat up. Or some ice cream? Or a pizza! Or maybe some tea?"

"We're okay for now, Mom," Ro said. "We'll just be working on some school stuff."

Ro's mom turned, her jewelry clinking. "Are you sure? I think we have some cookies around, if you need." She gathered up her purse. "I have to run to my open house. You kids will be fine, right?"

"Of course," Ro said.

"If you say so." Her mom swept her up in a one-armed hug and planted a kiss on her head.

Ro grinned and rubbed lipstick from her forehead. As her mom strapped on her heels and ran out the door, my chest felt a little tight. I mean, it wasn't like my mom didn't hug me—she hugged me plenty, mostly when she was worrying about me. But it was the way Ro and her mom almost melted into each other. Like butter or something. I wondered what her dad was like.

I looked around the kitchen. "What's up with all the plants?"

"Oh, that," Ro said, following my gaze. "My mom's just gotten into horticulture lately. See, there's her English ivy." She pointed to the leaves cascading down the window and almost into the sink. "And she's got some desert plants, too. Aloe and mini cactuses. And there are some orchids in the library that she's pretty proud of."

With the light coming in from the windows, her kitchen almost looked like a greenhouse. It was kind of cool, actually.

"Come on," Ro said. "The rocket's in the garage."

The garage, however, was an entirely different story. A bare bulb hung from the ceiling. There was a table with a bunch of tools on it. I recognized the bottle of gold paint she'd bought at Hogan's, along with the sandpaper and Popsicle sticks.

Ro walked over to the end of the table and fiddled around with what looked like a block with a lot of wires sticking out of it. She pressed a button, and the Doors streamed out, static and all.

"What," I asked, "is that?"

"My radio," she said, shrugging.

I stared at her in shock.

Honestly, who *builds* their own radio? Besides, I totally did not expect Ro to be into sixties rock. "Don't you guys have cassettes or something?"

"Yeah, but building your own radio is way cooler."

I shrugged.

"So this is my lab," Ro said, over the guitar intros. She looked over. "What do you think?"

I looked around at all the wires. "This looks exactly like a mad scientist's lab."

"Hey!"

"In a good way!" I put my hands up. I knew that all this stuff was *pretty* safe. It's just that whenever I thought of scientists, I always pictured the ones from my comics. Like how Dr. Bruce Banner put gamma rays through his body and then turned green and ballooned in size and became the Hulk. Or like how a lightning bolt hit Barry Allen's supplies, and then suddenly his body could travel at supersonic speed, and then he turned into the Flash.

I glanced around the room. It was pretty dimly lit. Cracks of sunlight streamed through the windows. The walls were a muted shade of brown. *If a lightning bolt hit Ro's radio—*

"Benji?"

I was getting *way*, way ahead of myself. "I mean, there's some cool stuff in here. Like your . . . radio thing." I walked over to the edge of the table, where there was a plastic cylinder surrounded by cut-out materials. "So this . . ."

"That's it," Ro said, coming around and fastening huge-looking lab goggles over her eyes. "It's the rocket. In progress."

"Whoa." It was bigger than I'd thought, with the top already put together. I looked at her in disbelief.

Ro Geraghty, the girl who sat next to me in class, was an actual, serious, live rocket scientist, goggles and all.

And she was actually trying to get a rocket up into space.

Mad Scientist Concocts Top-Secret Spaceship Rocket in Garage Lab!!!

"So these go into space?"

"Well, not *this* one," she said. She paused and picked up what looked like a tube and a mess of wires. "These are just model rockets. They only fly to a max of a couple thousand feet."

Still, that was way cool.

"You think you wanna get one to space someday?"

She nodded. "Absolutely."

I had no idea she was so serious about it. I mean, I didn't think it was a joke or anything—I'd seen her sketches stuffed with equations and those hieroglyphic-y math symbol things. I didn't know she actually wanted to launch a rocket, like those ones I saw on TV. Still, she sounded so confident that I actually kind of believed her.

"Okay," I said. "So how can I help?"

"Well," she said, coming over. "You have to know a couple of things about the rocket first."

She pointed to the top, the middle, and then the bottom, where one of the fins was jutting out. "Nose, airframe, fins. Airframe is the body of the rocket. I've trimmed the fins a little to make it fly higher. It's supposed to go over fifteen hundred feet, according to my calculations, but I think we can push it to sixteen." She pointed to the plan. "We're also going to add a radio transmitter in there"—she pointed to a mess of wires over at the end of the table—"to send signals back to the ground."

"You're building *another* radio?"

"Shouldn't be that hard," she said. "I mean, usually people just launch the rocket itself, but I wanted to add something to, you know, keep track of speed and how high it goes and all that. I was going to get a rocket camera, but that's too expensive to order. So I thought I'd just build a radio instead." She straightened up. "Anyway. The point is, if we stick to the plan, we'll be A-OK. Got it?"

"Yeah," I said, even if I didn't understand half of what she said. I looked at the rocket. "But hey, we should put some space blasters on this."

"What?"

"Wouldn't that be cool? Like if we were under attack, we'd be prepared. Oh, and we could add some forcefield shields while we're at it."

"That's impossible," she said curtly.

I looked down. *Jeez.*

"But," she said, grinning a little, "we could add on some sonic jet packs, just for some extra speed."

"Now we're talking."

"I'll consider it for the next prototype." She handed me the hammer. "Ready?"

Honestly, I'd never expected to get excited about a science project. It was just supposed to be a part of a deal, right? Ro would use her genius brain to think of ways to

71

track my dad down. I would put up with an hour here, maybe two, tops, scribbling out numbers until Ro knew just how bad I was at calculating things. I could help paint the rocket, if anything. I would do the least work possible to get my name on a science fair poster so Mom would get off my back and I could keep Mr. Keanan's art class. Win-win. Well, win mostly for me.

But as Ro grinned across the table with that wide smile that crinkled the corners of her eyes, her goggles huge on her face, and the Beatles hummed out of her janky radio, and as I joked about all the cool things we could possibly add to the rocket, I realized, *This isn't half-bad.*

This could actually be kind of fun.

I didn't get my first letter from Amir until the beginning of November. It came in a skinny envelope, and Mom made sure to personally hand it to me.

"I miss that kid," she said. It was true—she especially loved Amir and would constantly invite him over for dinner. She'd even insist he bring home a batch of her slightly overcrisped brownies. "Tell him I said hello."

"Will do," I said. I raced to my room and carefully tore the side open and shook the letter out.

Hey, Ben Franklin, Amir began, and I grinned at my old nickname. *Sorry for the prolonged wait. I've been so busy in my move that I'd lost track of time.*

I rolled my eyes at the word *prolonged*. Of course. I'd forgotten he was practically like a walking thesaurus.

I have to say, New Haven's like an entirely different world from Sacramento. First of all, our current house is way tinier than our old house. I have to share a room with two of my sisters. Can you even imagine? The third one's at college, so we don't see her as much anymore, but when she comes home to visit, it's all four of us in one room. Sometimes I can barely even hear myself think.

But other than that, I love this place. It just snowed here, and so the roofs and bushes and sidewalks were all covered with snow when we woke up last Saturday. And in our neighborhood they say that during Christmas, everyone decorates their yards with holiday lights, just like how it was in England when we used to live there. I'd forgotten how much I missed it, honestly. We're also just two hours away from New York City, so we're planning to visit next weekend. Maman says we might even be able to visit Niagara Falls over winter break.

I smiled a little.

My new school is so much better. People still give me strange looks or have trouble pronouncing my name. But they don't pick on me or pull pranks on me like Drew did. I also met these two guys in my class, Kenny Lin and the other's Alex Freeman. They're both really nice to me. They helped me out with my project in science class and then invited me to their robotics club that they started. We're trying to build one of those robotic arms that can carry objects to you. Isn't that cool? Anyway, Alex invites us over to his house a lot because he's an only child and his parents are never home, so whenever I want some peace and quiet, I just walk over to his place. His parents let him watch as much TV as he wants, too. My baba won't even let us watch thirty minutes.

Spacebound comics?

I wish I was able to get the latest issue, but I can't read them anymore. Maman found my stash and threw them all away. She's telling me that it's about time I started reading real books. Of course I think she's being too strict, but I can't really do anything about it. But it'll mostly be fine. I'm pretty busy anyway.

Anyway, I'm going to go and figure out how to make this robotic arm move. Please do tell me everything that's occurred since I've left. Looking forward to the next letter.

74

I set the letter on my bed. The door opened behind me, and Mom came in with a pile of laundry.

"Amir wrote me," I said.

"I saw." She set my folded shorts on the bed. "He adjusting okay?"

"Yeah," I said. *More than okay,* I thought, with a little funny feeling in my chest. He lived on the other side of the country. He got two new best friends. I mean, he didn't even read comics anymore.

I tried to push aside that funny feeling. There was so much to tell him—about Ro and how we finally had put together a solid plan to find my dad. I fished a blank piece of paper from my backpack and started writing.

CHAPTER NINE
RO

I SET A half-constructed rocket ignition system on our kitchen countertop. "Do you know anything about how to construct a closed circuit? I can't seem to get this to work."

After weeks of working on it, I'd finally hit a wall. I even tried asking Mom for help.

Mom peered quizzically at the wires for a good ten seconds. Finally, she sighed, looking up. "Baobao, I have no clue how to do this." She stood up. "You know, I like the idea of your rocket, but is it really safe to be"—she gestured to the wires—"playing with this kind of stuff?"

"It's just wires and stuff, Mom," I said. "I can figure it out."

"Maybe you can ask our neighbor about this."

I looked up. "You mean Mr. Voltz?"

"Yeah," she said. She adjusted her jade bracelet. "He was

a radiotelephone operator for the army. He probably knows more about circuits than I do." She lowered her voice and leaned in. "Ask nicely, though."

That was how I ended up on Mr. Voltz's porch. I brushed aside cobwebs and pressed the doorbell. And as I waited, I stared at the bright blue peeling paint on the walls. I heard one, two muffled barks from within. *Ruff, ruff.*

I realized that I'd never actually spoken to my next-door neighbor before. It was always Dad who'd gone over, to help paint his fence or help build something that Mr. Voltz absolutely couldn't figure out. He'd go, and sometimes from my bedroom window I'd hear them talking and laughing over the voices of Mr. Voltz's radio. Dad could talk to anybody. Mrs. Voltz was always the one I'd seen more of. Sometimes, she brought muffins to our house because she tried a bunch of recipes. She taught Mom how to make the perfect sourdough loaf. But after Mrs. Voltz got cancer, she came over less and less. Mom and Dad brought over meals to the hospital every week up until she passed away. Dad was the one who made the casseroles because Mom had never made a casserole in her life; she brought tofu soups instead.

After That Night, when we were still getting used to the fact that Dad was never coming back, Mr. Voltz showed up at our steps with a burnt casserole of his own. He could barely look us in the eye. "I'm sorry about Richard," he said gruffly. He turned and left.

It wasn't that I didn't like Mr. Voltz. It just wasn't easy

to talk to him. Some people were scared of him. The only time I saw him come out of his house was on the night Drew Balonik set off those fireworks, when he came out and started shouting at the top of his lungs until the fire department calmed him down. It was the only time I heard him say anything more than a sentence, let alone raise his voice.

Mr. Voltz peered down, staring at me suspiciously. His dog bounded up to greet me. "Easy, Ellie," he said to the dog. Then to me, he said, "Hey there, Rosalind." He sounded out the syllables of my name slowly. "What do you want?"

I cleared my throat and held out the wires. "Ro's just fine. Do you know anything about circuits?"

He frowned and stared at it for a while. A long while. And then finally he said, "What for?"

"A rocket," I said.

He stared at me with an unreadable expression, and for a minute I almost thought he was going to laugh in my face or slam the door. But he just said, "A rocket."

"Yeah," I said. "I've got most of it worked out, but I just can't figure out the ignition system," I said, before his expression could change. "And I have to figure out how to put the parts together to close the circuit, so the electricity goes all the way around in a loop—"

"I know what a circuit is," Mr. Voltz said curtly. "Come in. Let me take a look at this."

Ellie nudged against me affectionately as Mr. Voltz sat at his kitchen table. I threaded my fingers through her soft fur. She stared up at me with big brown eyes.

At least his dog liked me.

We sat in silence, mostly, as Mr. Voltz put on his glasses and peered at the wires. Past the worn sofa, the small TV was broadcasting the 49ers game.

"It's supposed to connect to the rocket," I said. "The idea is that you press the doorbell, and then the circuit closes and then it turns on the motor. And then the rocket launches." I mimicked a rocket taking flight with my hands.

Mr. Voltz didn't say anything. He just scowled at the wires.

"I got these parts from your store," I said.

"I know you did."

A long silence passed. The clock ticked on the wall.

I watched the game.

I stood up. "You know, I'll probably just figure it out by myself," I said hurriedly. "Sorry for making you—"

"The wires are connected wrong," Mr. Voltz said. He pointed to the battery. "You're supposed to connect this to the positive and this to the negative, and you switched it."

"But the *Handbook of Model Rocketry* said—"

"Trust me. I did this for ten years of my life," Mr. Voltz said. "If you botch the circuit, nothing happens. Or worse, something happens, and it isn't good."

I sat back. "Oh."

Ellie bounded up and put her paws on me, her tail

wagging. Mr. Voltz looked over at us, and I could see him almost smile.

He didn't look so scary anymore. Cheering erupted from the TV. I turned back to watch the game, and this time, I noticed the framed picture of Mr. Voltz with Mrs. Voltz on one of the bookshelves behind the TV, taken when they were younger. Mr. Voltz had his arm around her, and she looked up at him instead of at the camera. "That's a nice picture," I said.

Mr. Voltz saw what I was looking at. "It is," he said, his eyes softening. But he didn't say anything more. His jaw trembled, and I wondered if I'd said something I shouldn't have. After a moment, he cleared his throat and stood. "Anything else?"

I shook my head and gathered up the wires. "Not really."

"Come back if you have any more questions," he said, as I was about to push open his screen door. "Ellie seems to like you a whole lot."

I grinned. At least I knew he didn't hate me. "I will."

It was nice to have someone to eat lunch with.

For someone who didn't say anything to me at the science table for the first two weeks, Benji was surprisingly easy to sit with. Even if it took a whole month for us to start eating together. Eventually he figured out I was eating alone, and I figured out that he was sneaking off to eat lunch in the art room, and we decided to sit together one day after class. We'd occupied the corner table of the lunchroom ever since. It was quieter, and besides, if a food fight ever broke out, the odds were low we'd get caught in the crossfire.

He didn't talk much, and most of the time he spaced out in class, but once we started talking during lunch, I forgot that he'd ever been quiet. He was always putting together weird combinations of his lunch food (our conclusions: cheese went great with peanut butter, but combining Oreos with orange juice was awful). His brother was the baseball star of the high school team, but Benji couldn't care less about sports, even if he did go around wearing the kind of T-shirts you get for free at baseball tournaments because they were his brother's hand-me-downs. His brother had clearly handed down his baggy shorts too, which made Benji's legs look extra skinny. His alien and Russian space conspiracy stories sounded a little too scientifically impossible and ridiculous, but they were fun to try to disprove.

Really, he was just a floppy-haired goofball who could probably subsist on Red Vines until the end of time. He was actually a really good artist, too. Sometimes, when I looked over and saw him sketching, I saw how his expression changed and how his eyebrows knitted together. My notebook was covered with perfect notes; his was a mess of sketches that connected to one another. He drew faces on his sketches of plants and chemicals and gave them funny expressions. I almost laughed out loud in class a couple of times. But when he was truly concentrating, it was almost like magic. He could lean over and, with a few confident strokes of his pencil, he could bring something to life.

I saw him sketching when I came into the lunchroom today, but when he saw me his face lit up and he immediately shut his book. He offered a bag of Bugles. "Want some?"

I surveyed his lunch. Other than the Bugles, he had a ziplock baggie of cereal and some yogurt. "Is this all?"

He shrugged. "Hey, this is a balanced meal." He gestured to the ziplock bags. "Grains. Dairy." He pointed to the Bugles. "Vegetables. Because, you know. They're made of corn."

I offered him my carrots and he took one. "Come on," I said. "Take more."

"Can't. That's already too much," he said. "Plus, did you know that that if you eat too many carrots, you turn orange?"

"That's probably not true."

"Is too," he said. "Learned it in sixth-grade science class."

"You actually paid attention?"

Benji shrugged. "It happens."

"Not today, it didn't," I retorted. "I think Mr. Devlin actually caught you napping this time."

"Okay, I stayed up reading the latest issue of *The New Mutants* last night."

"You're hopeless."

"Hey, I'm not changing anytime soon." His expression shifted. "Anyway, I have to ask you a serious question."

"What?"

"How do you feel about cereal mixed with yogurt?"

CHAPTER TEN
BENJI

I'D BEEN TO so many baseball games that I knew a good hit when I heard one.

Danny was cranking them out when Mom and I pulled up to the batting cages after she took me to my dentist appointment. Usually, Mom would have rushed up to the fence and called him over to leave, but today, she just sat down at a nearby picnic table and watched.

I scooted onto the bench, running my tongue over my teeth. I could still taste the weird lumpy mint fluoride. I thought about my emergency stash of Red Vines sitting back in my room.

It was like rewinding a tape. The machine would shoot out the ball. Danny would wind up. Swing. And his bat would connect with the hurtling pitch, hitting it with a perfect, sweet, hollow *ping*.

Pitch. Wind-up.

Ping.

"You know he's getting recruited, right?"

I looked at Mom, who was freeing her hair from a tight bun, her lips pursed in her usual worried look. She was still wearing her lavender-patterned scrubs from the hospital, and they looked a size too big on her. She kind of looked out of place, right next to a batting cage and a skate park where the older teenagers usually hung out. I said, "By colleges?"

She nodded.

"But Danny's only a junior."

Mom looked at me. "That's when they start looking." Mom smoothed her frizzy hair back and secured it with a clip. She popped in an Altoid mint. She was obsessed with those. "They're going to start showing up to some games when the season starts. Maybe he can land a scholarship, even, if he keeps his grades up. College isn't getting cheaper these days."

Pitch.

Ping.

Mom's eyes were still on Danny as she said, "Speaking of grades, I've been meaning to talk to you. I chatted with your old science teacher the other day."

"From last year?"

She nodded, her earrings dangling. "We were just continuing our conversation from, well, last June. She really wanted to recommend you for some extra help this year."

Not this again. Just when I thought she'd forgotten. I mumbled, "I don't need extra study hall."

She turned to me. "Come on, Benji. We've talked about this. Your math grades haven't been so great this quarter. And you got that C in science last year."

"Well . . ." It wasn't my fault that Mr. Martin took points off every time he saw me drawing in class.

Mom said, "Benji, I'm not one to fret, but we have to do something about this."

Danny took a break; the *pings* stopped for a while. "I'm fine now," I said. "I'm getting better at things. Plus, my lab partner is really smart. I'm doing the science fair with her this year, and Mr. Devlin said he'd give extra credit for that."

The look on Mom's face was priceless. "You're doing a science fair project?"

I nodded. "Yup."

"Since when? And on what?"

"Since September. And we're building rockets."

Her eyebrows shot up another inch. "You're pulling my leg."

"I'm not! I swear. My lab partner's practically a genius. She's even drawn up all these complicated math equations and those diagram things." I shrugged. "I trust her."

"Oh, that's great." Mom started smiling, for real this time. The extra Benji-sponsored wrinkles faded. She sighed. "You know I want the best for you. I just—"

"I know." I knew what she was going to say. She just

wanted to not worry about me like she didn't have to worry about Danny. Danny, the star shortstop who could hit a line drive with his eyes closed. Danny, with his near-perfect grades and his girlfriend, Chelsea, and his probably-most-likely fancy college scholarship. Danny, who was probably going to drive off into the sunset in his beat-up blue Ford, like Superman on his Supermobile.

Here's something Mr. Keanan taught me during his drawing unit in art class: details bring things to life. During lunch breaks, I'd be reading my comics and he'd be sketching different things, like a drawing of his guitar, or his dog, or his two kids. He'd start out with rough brush strokes and hone in. And suddenly, he'd lean over and with a few confident strokes of his pencil, he could add in a sly expression, or a twinkle in the eye, and bring someone to life.

Turns out, when you draw someone, you happen to notice things about them that other people don't. Like how when Mom was really, really happy, her eyes crinkled at the corners. Or how her left eye twitched if she was about to blow her top over something. Or how Drew Balonik twirled his pencil when he was about to pull a prank. Or how Amir cracked his knuckles when he had to speak in public, because talking in front of people made him super nervous. For Ro, it was easy to draw the blue-and-white windbreaker, or the clunky watch she wore on her right hand because she wrote with her left, or how she always pulled her wavy hair up in a half bun with her white hair tie. But it was harder to capture how she scrunched her face and stuck her tongue out a little when she was concentrating. Or how she brightened when she figured out how to get her radio to broadcast the Giants game.

Details like these matter in comic books. Characteristics are exaggerated. Even the slightest expressions are magnified. But sometimes you have to be picky about which details to draw, or whether to include them at all. Because how detailed a character is drawn depends on how important they are, really.

Like how in every action scene Captain Gemma Harris was in—whether she was bounding off of the hood of a spaceship or landing a powerful kick midspace—I could see the exact detail of her space suit down to the belt hooks and wrist cuffs and the beads of sweat on her face. Plumes of fires and stars whirled around her. Meanwhile, her crew members Asher and Falcon stared on, roughly drawn, with the only detail being the shocked expressions on their faces. The more important someone was, the more colorfully and detailed they were drawn.

Danny started swinging again. As I watched him wind up over and over, I couldn't stop thinking about what things would be like if that were true in real life. What if some people were lit up brightly, while others slipped by in the background?

Truth be told, if my life were a comic book, my brother would probably be the hero. I could even see it. His helmet would be bright red. I could picture the detail of his base-ball jersey and the sheen of sweat carefully sketched in and the pencil catching his laser focus while he struck out another player. Imagine that, on the front page of the news-paper, captured in vivid colors. Mom would tack it up on the fridge with her circular magnet clips.

And, well, maybe it was always gonna be like that. Some people would always be made of bright reds and blues and flashes and those *BANG* and *KAPOW* symbols and all that fun stuff. And I would be that sweet sidekick in the background. Or something. With my Red Vines. Barely sketched out and barely shaded in.

CHAPTER ELEVEN
RO

"I'M CONFUSED," BENJI said as he slowed down so I could catch up. "This whole town is flat as a board. Why do we need to find some special place on your map again?"

"We can't just fire off a rocket from any old place," I said. "Think about it. What if we accidentally launched it into a telephone pole?"

"You don't get your calls?"

"*And* you could shut down the power on your entire street," I said. "Or set something on fire."

"The power going out is actually pretty scary," Benji said. "I mean, the fire, too. But my neighbors would really go nuts if they didn't get to watch *Jeopardy!* at seven every night."

We pulled up to a field, and I double-checked the map. This was it. There was a faded soccer goalpost, but it was at the end of the field, near the park. I scanned around. The closest house was hundreds of feet to the left. Nothing. Zip. Zero.

Just grass.

"Well," Benji said. "I don't think we could set anything on fire here if we tried."

We set down our rocket. I turned back. So we'd found a place. *Check.* "Okay. We can just find a spot to—"

"Aw, come *on.*"

I looked up.

I instantly recognized Drew Balonik, with his spiky brown hair and his red hoodie. He smiled like he was playing some big joke that we didn't even know about. Two other kids followed him. One of them was Eddie, Drew's friend in science class who always laughed at everything Drew said. The other one I'd only seen a few times at lunch.

Benji tapped on my shoulder. "We should probably go."

But Drew had already come up to us. "Hey."

I noticed Benji clench his fists. His cheeks were red.

"Nice seeing you, Burns," Drew said. He smiled, but it didn't look friendly at all. "Didn't expect you here."

Observation: Benji and Drew hated each other.

"What are *you* doing here?" Benji said. His cheeks were still bright red.

"I live here, moron," Eddie said.

"We were tossing a Frisbee when we saw you biking by," Drew said. "We just wanted to say hi, that's all."

His friends laughed. Benji looked away. "Come on," he mumbled to me. "Let's go."

But I didn't particularly feel like leaving. I wanted to wipe that stupid smirk off Drew's face. I marched right up to him. "Hey. Leave us alone."

Drew looked surprised. "Hey, it's the new girl." He looked between us and raised his eyebrows. "*Ohhh.* Were we interrupting a date?"

Benji turned three shades redder. "What! I mean—no. That's not—"

"Aw, don't be *embarrassed*," Drew said in a mocking voice. "Benji Burns and his—"

"We're here to test out our science fair experiment, actually," I said loudly, stepping right in front of him. "And you're messing it up."

Drew doubled over laughing. "Science fair?" I didn't really know what was funny. "You're—doing all this for"— he straightened up—"the *science fair?*"

Before I knew it, he'd snatched the rocket. "What is this, a big stick?" He turned. "Andrew, catch!"

He threw it like it was a football, and Andrew ran down the field, catching it with both hands.

"Hey!" I ran after his friend Andrew, but he tossed it back, and Drew caught it. Panic rose and then boiled over into anger as Drew tumbled to the ground roughly, rolling over with the rocket. A part of the fin wobbled, nearly snapping off.

Benji didn't do a thing. He just stood by his bike, watching the whole thing happen. But I wasn't going to let Drew ruin this. I'd spent *months* on that rocket.

"Let's fly this like a paper airplane!" Drew said, swinging the rocket around. "Maybe we can get it in—*uufff*!"

I'd meant to only grab the rocket, but I accidentally toppled right on top of Drew and we both tumbled to the ground. I wrenched the rocket away from him, scrambling to my feet.

"Hey!" Drew protested. "You pushed me!"

"I didn't mean to," I said. "Anyway, what are you going to do, tell on me?"

He opened his mouth and shut it.

"You know what?" I spat out. "You might think you're funny with those stupid jokes you make in class. Or with all the times you fling Jell-O in someone's face. But it's not funny to me. So you can get up and leave now," I said. "And for your information, my name is Ro. Don't call me new girl."

Drew got up, stunned. He didn't say anything for a second. "Okay, freako, chill out," he said, giving me a nasty look. He glanced at his friends. "Come on, leave these nerds to their stupid science experiment."

As they headed back, I turned to Benji. His mouth was open.

"I can't believe you did that. That was *amazing*!"

I was still angry. "I can't believe he goes around doing that to people."

Benji shrugged. "He always gets a laugh out of it."

I didn't say anything for a while. "Does he not like you or something?"

"Our brothers are friends," Benji said.

I whirled around. "What?"

"Yeah. I used to go to his house sometimes. But then he started playing a bunch of pranks on people, and I didn't really want to be friends with him. He likes that kind of stuff. Jokes and pranks. He also made fun of my old friend Amir a lot. So I don't really like him."

It occurred to me that Drew probably used to make fun of Benji, too. "I just made him hate you more, didn't I?"

"Well, Drew hates both our guts now," Benji said. And then he cracked the biggest smile I'd seen. "But that was *totally* worth it."

CHAPTER TWELVE
BENJI

SO HERE'S THE thing: Drew Balonik and I used to be best friends.

I know.

I just repeated that again in my head, because to be honest, I wouldn't have believed myself in a million years, either. And I wasn't just friends with him for a week or a month or something; we were best friends ever since kindergarten, when Drew marched up to me in my Little League game with his oversized jersey and his spiky hair, and said, "My brother told me to be friends with you."

I mean, why wouldn't I? Drew's brother Ellis came over to our house to play with Danny so much that their names kind of blended together, like *Dannyellis*. So Drew started coming over. I went over to his house a lot, too. His parents were real nice and always bought Drew the newest gadgets.

He even got his own Walkman for his twelfth birthday. We started sitting together at lunch. He gave me half of his Fruit Roll-Up. I gave him some Red Vines. When we were finally in the same class together, Drew told me to learn Morse code so he could talk to me during reading hour by just blinking. And on April Fools' Day of fifth grade, Drew brought a whoopee cushion to class because Ellis had tricked him with it. When Mrs. Farnsworth wasn't looking, he slipped it onto her seat. And when she finally sat down—

FFFFT.

The class roared with laughter. After that everyone wanted to sit with Drew at lunch.

And then three things happened during sixth grade:

I quit baseball.

Drew told me his mom and dad started fighting a lot.

He got brand-new Nikes and a book of practical jokes for his birthday.

A lot of jokes were kind of dumb. They involved squirting ketchup between your fingers and pretending it was blood, or having someone step in a puddle of shaving cream. But everyone else at school loved it. When we sat together at lunch, they squealed and *oohed* and *aaahed* over the fake-ketchup-hot-sauce blood. Once, Drew pulled out a jar of mayonnaise and started eating straight from it with a spoon, and everyone said it was gross until Drew told them it was actually pudding.

Two weeks into sixth grade, Drew pulled me aside after class. "Hey. I think I just started a prank war with some eighth graders."

My heart rate shot up. *"What?"* The eighth graders were *huge*. They had tree trunks for legs.

"Hey, chill," Drew said. "They pulled a joke on me in the hallway, so I'm gonna get them back. Help me put together a list of good pranks, will you?"

The next day, the entire school was talking about how Evan Hamm opened his locker and a sea of Styrofoam peanuts spilled out.

They stopped messing with Drew pretty quick after that. But he still continued with his Prank Wars, even though it was no longer a war.

And I admit, almost all the pranks that Drew came up with were pretty funny. Like when he taped a harmonica to the back of the principal's car so that when he started his car after school, the harmonica screeched loud enough for the sheriff to hear. Or when he snuck into homeroom early, when all the chairs were put up, and duct-taped them to the desks so people couldn't sit down for class. Or when he used the pay phone near the principal's office and kept prank calling our math teacher (which was my idea) until the entire class was roaring with laughter.

But when Drew offered me one of his mom's caramel apples and I took a huge bite of a caramel-covered onion instead, it wasn't all that funny. He and our other friends cracked up at my horrified reaction. I choked down the caramel onion and tried to smile, too. But mostly, their laughter just made me feel kind of awful. Or maybe it was the raw onion.

"I should put Mrs. Lewis's paper clips in Jell-O on the last day before winter break!" Drew said, lying on my floor and staring at the ceiling while I concentrated on drawing Superman. We hung out only at my house now. He had the bigger house, with its shiny new countertops and its matching drapes. But his parents fought so much Drew didn't like being home. "But maybe that's not big enough. I gotta pull out all the stops."

I put down my drawing. "Haven't you done enough pranks?"

"Are you kidding?" Drew said. If I had to draw him, I would pencil in sparks and angry cyclones around him. That was Drew: he was always causing some sort of trouble. "I'm just getting started. People love these things. Eddie told me that my pranks make him actually *want* to go to school. Come on, put down those stupid comics and gimme some ideas."

It was true. People always laughed along with his pranks.

Until the middle of sixth grade, when a small, skinny kid named Amir showed up in science class. His green checkered shirt seemed to swallow him up. His hair was perfectly combed. It was the day of the Pepsi prank. The teacher, Mr. Martin, always drank a bottle of Pepsi without fail, and so we thought that one day, we'd wait until he wasn't looking and put a bunch of Pop Rocks in it.

Mr. Martin was busy passing around the beakers when Drew snuck up to his desk.

And then he paused for a moment, as if thinking about it. Silently, he moved the Pepsi bottle just slightly to the right and placed it behind Amir, who was standing closest to the desk, his back turned to the Pepsi.

My stomach did a cartwheel. "Wait—"

Too late. When Amir wasn't looking, Drew slipped a bunch of Pop Rocks in the bottle. Instantly, the soda exploded all over the new kid.

I couldn't laugh. I couldn't smile, not even a tiny bit. I remembered Drew and our other friends laughing when Drew played pranks on me and knew it must have been ten times more awful for the new kid.

During lunch, when I saw Amir sitting alone with Pepsi stains on his collared shirt, picking at his lunch, I felt like I was going to throw up.

I didn't even know him then, really. But the thing was, I'd always read all about these characters in my comics.

Bruce Wayne snuck out as Batman at night and protected innocent strangers from crime. Superman went around saving people.

And I couldn't even stop a new kid from getting pranked on his first day of school. It finally hit me: I didn't want to do pranks anymore.

"I got it!" Drew said to me after school that day. "I finally got an idea for the Big Prank. I'm going to put all the fish from the principal's fish tank into the science beakers just in time for our class experiment! They'll go nuts over this."

I could not believe what I was hearing. He was going to mess with the *goldfish*?

"They're live creatures," I protested.

"So? Come on, man, they're just goldfish. I'll put in some water from the fish tank, too. You think it'll be funny?"

I stood up.

What I wanted to say was: "I'm out."

What I said instead was: "Yeah, course."

But the next day, all I kept thinking about was Amir and his Pepsi-stained shirt. I felt more and more awful, until it was like I had the worst flu ever.

Was it possible to throw up by just thinking about something?

Which was how I ended up in the principal's office the first time.

After I told them all about how Drew was going to fill the beakers with the goldfish from the tank during the lunch break, Mr. Murphy stormed into the science room and found Drew reaching into the fish tank.

Which is how I ended up in the principal's office the second time, while Drew's face got all red and he burst into tears.

That was how the Prank Wars ended.

And how Drew stopped talking to me.

Because I got him in trouble.

And worse, the school called his mom.

And worse, he got detention for two weeks.

But worst of all, I was a big, fat, lying snitch.

Because the first rule of friendship was: no matter what, friends don't tell on each other.

I felt awful being a snitch. But the thing was, I'd felt worse and worse every time Drew pulled a prank, and if I hadn't stopped it, I genuinely think I would have puked my guts out. Drew still pulled some harmless jokes after detention, because after all, people still laughed at his pranks. But he never pulled a prank on me again.

Still, after what Ro had done to Drew in the park, I wasn't sure how safe Ro was. I didn't hear anything from her the next day. But I did hear about how someone had planted spiders—fake spiders—all over Mrs. Campbell's desk.

I leaned over the counter. "But I thought the new issue was coming today?"

Mr. Voltz peered at me from over his glasses. "Back-ordered.

It'll come the next two weeks, maybe. I'll let you know."

I sighed. I'd biked all the way to school for this instead of hitching a ride with Danny, just so I could bike here after. Danny wasn't working today.

So, it was just me and Caterpillar Eyebrows.

As I was about to go back to the comics aisle, he said, "Patience, young man. You know, I wait to stock those space comics until you've come so others won't get to them first."

I looked up. "Really?" He *saved* those comics so I could get to them first? It was practically the nicest thing I'd ever heard. "I feel bad now," I said. "I don't even end up buying them sometimes."

I could see him almost smiling. *Almost.* He nodded. "Doesn't matter. I don't mind you reading them, as long as you don't mess them up. Anyway, kids usually come in for *Batman.* Or for those Marvel issues. Seems like that's what everyone likes these days." He peered at me. "What *is* it about these *Spacebound* books that do it for you, anyway?"

I shrugged, trying to think of some excuse. Then, without thinking, I blurted out, "My dad writes those comics, actually. That's why."

Mr. Voltz's expression didn't change. Not even a tiny smidge. "Oh?"

"Yeah. I found drawings around the house that he did. Before he left, probably. These comics came out years after he left. But the stuff he drew matched up to those comics exactly. I don't think Mom knows. Or Danny. They don't

102

read *Spacebound*. But I do."

I paused. *Why was I blabbing on about this?* But now that I'd started, I couldn't really stop. Plus, I actually felt okay about trusting Mr. Voltz. It wasn't like he would tell anyone, anyway. "The thing is, everyone loves *Star Wars*. But *Spacebound* feels like my own comic because my dad wrote it, you know? I don't remember what he sounds like. Mom won't talk about him, ever. She doesn't even keep pictures of him around the house, so I don't even know what he really looks like. But when I read *Spacebound*, it's like I can figure it out a little. I can see what jokes he likes to make. Almost like I can hear him talking." I looked up, suddenly feeling self-conscious. I'd probably told him too much. "Sorry, this probably sounds all super weird."

But Mr. Voltz shook his head. "Not at all."

I said, "I want to find him, though." *There.* I'd said it. And somehow, this mission to look for my dad felt more real, because I was telling all this to an adult. Who, before today, was practically a stranger. "I want to know what he's really like. So my friend Ro and I are looking for him."

I expected him to raise an eyebrow or scoff at the idea or shake his head, but he simply nodded. He reached for his pillbox on the counter and shook it out.

I glanced over. "You take vitamins, too?"

Mr. Voltz paused. "You think these are vitamins?"

"Aren't they? I mean, they kinda look like the vitamins that Mom makes me take. 'Cause she's always flipping out

about whether I get enough vitamin D or B or something."
I peered at them. "If they aren't vitamins, what are they?"

Mr. Voltz tipped up the pills and swallowed them all at
once. He took a sip from his glass of water. "Medicine."

"Do you have a cold?"

He paused, like I was testing his patience. "It's for my
bad nerves," he finally said.

"What bad nerves?"

His smile was gone. He fixed me with a stern look.
"Quit asking so many questions."

"Sorry," I said. We didn't really say anything else. Maybe
I was talking too much. Or maybe I shouldn't have asked.
I turned and went back to the comics shelves.

"What does it mean to have bad nerves?" I asked at dinner.

Danny was out having dinner at Chelsea's house, so it
was just Mom and me. She'd heated up some leftover SpaghettiOs, but Mom always overdid it with the microwave,
so they were still burning hot.

Mom looked up. "What?"

"Mr. Voltz. He told me he has bad nerves. He takes pills
for it, too."

"Oh, *that*." Mom sighed. "It's not bad nerves. Or that's
not what doctors call it anyway. Mr. Voltz has something
called battle fatigue."

"Oh," I said, but I still didn't really know what that
meant. I took a bite of my SpaghettiOs and practically

breathed fire out my mouth. *Ow, hot.* "Is that why people say he gets fits?"

"They're not *fits,* Benji. It's rude to call them that."

"Everyone says that!"

"He just gets anxious sometimes, that's all," Mom said. Under the harsh light of the kitchen, I could see that her worry lines were back. She smoothed back her hair, and then it poufed up all around her again in a reddish mane. "A lot of men his age get that way. They went through some awful things when they were off fighting those wars in World War II and Korea. Sometimes the war stays with them. Mrs. Voltz told me he still gets nightmares about it from time to time. They get startled easily, too." She looked pointedly at me. "Like when your friend had the *brilliant idea* to set off those fireworks, for example—"

"He's not my friend anymore," I mumbled. "We haven't hung out in months."

Mom paused. I knew she never really liked Drew; he never got a batch of her brownies. "Oh. I guess I knew. I wondered why he'd stopped coming around the house. Well, I'm glad. I don't want you associating with trouble-makers like that. Those fireworks sounded like machine guns, you know. They probably scared the living daylights out of Mr. Voltz."

"I didn't know that."

"Not a lot of people do. They don't like talking about it, these veterans. It's been years since they fought in a war, and people are still coming into the hospital for the first time for treatment because all these years they thought it was something an aspirin could fix. It's good he's taking pills for it at least. His wife made sure of that."

I'd known that he was a veteran, but he never talked about the war.

Now I knew why. I looked down at my mushy Spaghet-tiOs. I thought of Drew and his friends calling him a spaz and felt sick to my stomach.

CHAPTER THIRTEEN
RO

"WHAT IF THIS thing doesn't stop flying and then escapes into the sky?" Benji said as I perched the rocket launcher carefully on the grass. "Like one of those big helium balloons that you accidentally let go of?"

"Not possible," I said. "We put a parachute in there, remember? Once the rocket starts coming down, the engine's going to push out the parachute to slow down the descent. But hey, if this thing goes off to space on the first try, then I'd say it was a success." I stacked the rocket on the launch rod and then stepped back.

Benji just said, "Wow."

I looked it up and down. This was it. The first rocket launch. Well, technically, the first *official* rocket launch, since Drew had derailed our planned launch a couple of days ago. Benji and I had spent a whole afternoon fixing the fin that Drew had bent. I stared at the rocket, and the trail of wires coming out of it that would snap off as it took flight. In the back of my mind, I remembered the guy at the hobby store Dad and I visited telling me that this might take a couple of tries to get right. But still, I couldn't help but stare at the rocket we'd spray-painted red and blue and gold and be hopeful. It wasn't named *Expedition* after Gemma Harris's spaceship for nothing. And for a second I pictured it hurtling off, far enough into space, far enough to cross galaxies and—

"Hey," Benji said, snapping his fingers. "Are we launching this thing, or are you just going to make googly eyes at it?"

Right. We were launching.

"Should I make this more realistic?" Benji said. He mimicked holding a microphone. "Reporting live from NASA . . ."

I laughed. "Just stand back."

I looked around. Everything was clear. I double-checked that we had everything. The rocket, with the parachute and the radio transmitter inside, was propped up on the launch rod. The ignition system was wired to the engine. All I had to do was press the doorbell button, and the circuit would be closed and the timer would start counting down. My walkie-talkie was clutched in my hand so I could receive signals from the transmitter. "Two things to watch for," I said. "Rocket should reach about sixteen hundred feet high at its apogee. I'll pay attention to the walkie-talkie to see if we can hear any signals. If both things happen . . ."

"It'll be a *smashing* success." Benji nodded. "Copy that."

"The countdown is ten seconds," I said. "We press the button, count to ten, and then . . ."

"*Pffssshhhh*." Benji mimicked a rocket taking off.

"Exactly," I said. I looked at him and felt a thrill of excitement. "Ready?"

He nodded.

I leaned forward and pushed down.

Ten.

Nine.

Eight.

Seven.

My palms were starting to feel clammy. I looked over the plans, at the drawings and calculations, seeing the familiar numbers again and again.

Did NASA astronauts feel like this, too?

Dad would love this.

Four.

Three.

Two.

One.

There wasn't a deafening boom. There wasn't a huge supersonic clap of sound. But there was a pop, a *SHHHHHH*, and—

My rocket was off.

I, Rosalind Ling Geraghty, had just launched a rocket.

One Mississippi, two Mississippi, three Mississippi—

It was still going.

I snapped pictures, my fingers shaking in disbelief. Frantically, I lowered the camera and hurriedly measured the current height with my homemade optical tracker. Two hundred feet and counting.

Ecstatic, I set the tracker device down and turned away from the rocket to see Benji's reaction. His mouth was hanging open. He whistled. "Well, genius."

And then it was as if some spell were broken. I grabbed his shoulders. "We did it! We really did it! Okay. Now we just wait ten more seconds for the rocket to reach coasting altitude! And then after it deploys the parachute and lands, we'll record the height and time and compare them to our predict—"

Benji's expression changed. "Uh, Ro?"

He pointed behind me.

The rocket wasn't coasting. It was already falling, fast, wobbling in the air. My heart plummeted into my gut. A mess of static blared out from the walkie-talkie, instead of clear radio signals.

No, no, no—

Expedition hurtled toward the ground. The nose cone flew off, and there was a *fwwp* as the parachute billowed out, catching the rocket midflight to break the fall.

I sprinted all the way over to where the rocket had

landed. It was supposed to land all the way across the field, and it only got halfway. The nose cone was missing, the parachute a tangle of plastic and string. The transmitter had tumbled out. One of the fins was almost falling off.

This couldn't be right. It should have taken longer. Way longer. I grabbed a piece of paper from my legal pad and quickly jotted down some numbers.

How were we so, so off?

Here's what should have happened: the rocket was supposed to launch straight up and reach maximum speed within seconds. It was supposed to reach an altitude of 1,620 feet, give or take 20 feet, at its apogee, or its highest point. It was supposed to stay airborne for twenty-six seconds before the recovery mechanism deployed. That was the Plan.

Dad always said to have a Plan for everything.

Here's what happened: the rocket stayed airborne for twenty seconds. It reached a maximum height of barely 400 feet.

"Well," Benji said. I could tell he was trying to keep his voice upbeat. "Not bad for our first attempt."

I looked down at the rocket. I swallowed and my throat felt tight. I nodded, not looking up. "Not bad," I repeated numbly.

But I hadn't been going for not bad.

I had been going for perfect.

CHAPTER FOURTEEN
BENJI

UPDATE ON THE Mission to Reunite Benji with His Long-Lost Father: we were stuck.

Really, really stuck.

"So I finally read the part where she finds out where her dad is," Ro said. She started looking through the comics again. She handed me a stack of comics, except now the pages were littered with sticky notes everywhere. "And I took some notes."

I stared at what seemed like a million Post-it edges peeking between the pages. "Are you doing this for a grade or something?"

"I wanted to be thorough," Ro said. "You're welcome, too."

"Thanks," I mumbled. "You did this a lot better than I would have." I probably would have flipped through the comics to look for clues and then gotten distracted by the story. And before I knew it, I'd be rereading all of volume 2 with a flashlight at night.

"I caught up with everything because I couldn't take you spoiling the story anymore."

"And you wanted to find out how Gemma escaped that trap," I said. "Imagine waiting an entire *four months* after that cliffhanger. Amir and I even made up a list of possible ways Gemma could have escaped, just to make the wait more bearable." Some ideas were more realistic, like finding some way to call for backup from the raiders. Other ideas involved inventing some kind of gamma-ray explosion that would shatter the cave walls and paralyze the bad guys.

Needless to say, neither of us got anywhere close.

"Have you told your friend about this?" Ro waved to our haphazard pile of atlases, comic books, and candy wrappers.

"Yeah, I wrote about it in my last letter," I said.

"What'd he think?"

I shrugged. "I don't know. Hasn't replied yet. He'll probably write when he has time." I didn't know when he ever would. I imagined him biking up a street, with each house decked with holiday lights. At this moment, he was probably working on making robot arms or whatever else he was doing with his new friends. He didn't even read comics anymore.

"You could call him," Ro pointed out.

"He's in *Connecticut*." I sighed, pushing a breath out between my lips. "Can you imagine how much it'd cost to make a long-distance call across the country? My mom would never let me call out of state."

I wondered what it was like to have a normal dad who wasn't impossible to contact. A dad who showed up. I wondered what Ro was like with her dad. Come to think of it, she didn't mention him much, but I'm sure they at least ate dinners together.

"Yeah, I guess I really never thought about it," Ro said, carefully tearing a PayDay wrapper. "Everyone I know is from California at least. I can't imagine ever leaving the state."

"Says the girl who wants to go to Mars," I muttered.

Ro grinned. "Okay, I'll probably have to leave the state *sometime*." She turned back to the June issue of *Spacebound* and flipped through the pages. "By the way, you know they're making a movie out of this, right?"

"Uh-huh," I said, pulling out my carton of Red Vines. I opened the atlas and flipped through it. "They announced it on the back cover of the last issue, right? But I don't know when it's coming out."

"It will be incredible, though, when it does," Ro said, reaching for a Red Vine. "But anyway, I looked at all the scenes on Earth and compared them to the cities on our list." She shook her head. "It's just impossible to narrow down. I looked at all the pictures on the atlas, too.

The desert parts look like Arizona, but they could also be New Mexico. The cities on Earth? There's no way to tell. It could be New York or Chicago or Los Angeles." She sighed and then reached for the atlas. "I think we've hit a wall."

Like I said, stuck.

"Well." I stared at pictures of the New York skyline. I said, half-jokingly, "We could just sit here eating Red Vines until we figure something out."

Ro stared at the wall for a while. "The rest of the book just takes place in outer space," she muttered to herself. She looked at me. "Do you think she'll return to Earth anytime soon?"

"I doubt it," I said. "I mean, we know her origin story now, right? She discovered that she's actually from the planet Scion but was brought to Earth by accident, and then adopted and raised there. So wouldn't Scion technically be her home planet?"

And then—

Boom. There it was.

The idea practically *crashed* into me.

"What if—" I paused. "What if we're looking in the wrong place?"

Ro frowned. "What do you mean?"

"If Earth isn't her home planet, and Scion is . . ."

Ro's eyes lit up. "Then we should be looking at Scion, not Earth!"

I flipped to the part where Gemma arrived on the planet. The skyline looked familiar for some reason, but I couldn't tell . . .

Ro said, "It's New York."

She turned the atlas around.

I scanned the picture of the skyline, where the Empire State Building looked exactly like . . .

The Scion Central in *Spacebound*.

"Okay," I said. I swear, my heart was beating at supersonic speed. "We need more. Is there like a subway system or something—?"

"There is, but it's not just that," Ro said breathlessly. She smacked her forehead with her palm. "How did I not realize to look here? It *has* to be New York."

"Huh?"

"The Dignitary Statue!" Ro pointed to the edge of the drawing of Scion I'd missed when I first read it. Anyone could have missed it.

But now that I saw it, it stared me in the face.

"Just like the Statue of Liberty," I said.

It was a perfect match.

We weren't crazy. My dad had actually, genuinely been leaving clues for us all this time.

I looked at Ro. Ro looked at me.

"Well, partner," she said. "We might have just figured it out."

★ ★ ★

I was still thinking about New York that night when Danny opened my door a crack. "Hey. Got a sec?"

He sat at the foot of my bed. The springs creaked.

I pulled my blankets up to my chin. Huh. Danny wasn't the type to stop by for a nightly chat. Besides, he usually stayed up cramming in his homework after his Hogan's shifts or his games. Or, since we were on winter break and didn't have homework, he'd be hogging the phone calling his girlfriend or something. Or one of his friends. I couldn't tell who he was talking to. I'd just heard him raising his voice in the next room over, as if in a heated argument.

Why was he coming to talk? I tried to think of what I could possibly have done but came up blank. "Whatcha want?"

"Nothing, Bo," he said. I hadn't heard my nickname in a while. "I've just been busy. We haven't, you know, talked. Besides, you weren't at the store today. Mr. Voltz told me to give you this."

He held out the new issue of *Spacebound*.

I sat straight up in bed. "You bought it?"

"Nah, he just gave it to me. Said it was paid for. Told me to wish you a merry Christmas."

My heart rose. I couldn't keep from grinning. The front cover was smooth, the pages new and crisp and glossy. No creases or bent edges. I hugged it to my chest. Danny grinned at me. I looked up. "Who were you just calling?"

"Chelsea." He sighed. "We've been fighting some." He

ran his hand through his hair. "I'm sure it'll be fine, though. We always figure it out."

"Oh," I said. Danny never told me anything about his girlfriend, but I always saw her at his baseball games and he always went to her soccer games, and when they weren't going to each other's games they were going on ice cream dates to Vic's. They were so nice to each other in front of me, I just assumed they never fought.

Plus, Mom adored Chelsea, and Mom only actually likes probably fifteen people. Mom wasn't the kind of person who baked cookies for everyone on the block, but when she liked you, she made sure you knew it.

"I'm sorry I've been away so much," Danny said, looking down the floor. "I've been training like crazy. And the coaches have been recruiting us, too."

"Schools are coming to see you?"

"You bet," Danny said. "It's the most nerve-wracking thing, I swear. You know USC? The one in LA? I picked up one of their pamphlets the other day, and jeez, it's just such a cool place. Sunny with palm trees and all that. But apparently it's super hard to get recruited by them."

"I'm sure you'll get it."

"I mean, it probably doesn't matter," Danny said. "I'll take any college that gives me money." He looked up with a hint of a smile. "Anyway. So Mom told me you're in the science fair now. How'd you get caught up in that?"

I laughed. "I did it to get out of that extra tutoring class."

Danny nodded. "Okay, I can take that. You doing okay without your friend?"

Without Ro? *Oh, he meant Amir.* I nodded. "Wrote him a letter a while ago. He hasn't responded, though."

"And who's that new friend of yours? Ray?"

"Ro," I said.

"Like the sport?"

I rolled my eyes. "R-O," I spelled out.

Dan raised his eyebrows. "Are you two—"

"No," I cut in. "Gross."

"You sure?"

"Positive," I said. There was no chance of that. Ze-ro. I'd been around Drew enough to know that going out in middle school just meant obnoxious note passing for weeks at a time. Or, worse yet, bad spin-the-bottle games. Plus, a solid perk of being his friend was that no girl ever even glanced my way. "We don't make kissy faces like you and Chelsea do."

"We do *not*," Danny said, his cheeks turning pink.

"Do too."

"We just like hanging out with each other. That's all." His eyes flickered up. "But I miss hanging out with you, too."

"It's not like we live in the same house or something," I said.

Danny smiled a little bit. "Anyway," he said. He cleared his throat. "There's something else I wanted to talk to you about. I thought you might want this." He handed over a sheet of paper.

Mission to Reunite Benji with His Long-Lost Father.

I sat straight up and snatched it. "You took this from my room?"

"I found it at the dinner table, okay? You're lucky I got to it before Mom did." He paused. His voice was sharp. "You're trying to find Dad?"

"Danny, Dad wrote these comics," I said. "He's out there somewhere."

Danny said, "I know."

"You *knew*?"

"I've known for a while now. I found one of his drawings with my old report cards. I didn't really think much about it until I started shelving those comics for Hogan's. And then I kind of put two and two together."

He had got to be kidding me. Danny *knew*?

"Why didn't you ever tell me? *Amir* was the one who told me!"

Danny looked down. "It wouldn't have changed anything."

"It would have changed everything!"

My brother narrowed his eyes. "Are you actually tracking him down?"

"So what if I am?" I threw back. "Did you know that Dad put clues in his comics to tell us where he is? Ro and I figured it all out. Dad lives in New York, Danny. New

York! Don't you want to see him? We could go together."
I rushed on. "And I know that this probably won't make
Mom happy, but—"

"It's not just that," Danny said flatly.

"Then what?"

Danny shrugged. "Believe me, Bo. I tried. But there's
just no point to finding him."

I felt sick. I practically *knew* where Dad was, probably,
and my brother didn't care. Anger rose. I couldn't help
snapping, "You don't even care, do you? Of course you
wouldn't."

"What do you mean?" Danny's voice was sharp.

"I mean, it's not like you'd need Dad around, anyway." I
shot back. "Come on, Danny. Mom loves you. Jeez, Chelsea and all your friends and your entire school are all *in love
with you.* Your life is perfect as is. Why would you even care
about Dad?"

"Of course I care!" Danny retorted. "You don't think I
care that when it's my senior night at my baseball game and
everyone's mom and dad walks their kid out, only my mom
is going to walk me down? You don't think I have to listen
to Mom worry about *everything* from whether she's working enough hours to her taxes to whether she should start
dating again, not just whether I clean my room or not? You
don't think I have to hold down a job on top of baseball
on top of knowing that the only way I'm going to college
is through a baseball scholarship, because there's no other

way we could afford it?" He paused. "You don't think I miss him too? Come on, Benji. I used to cry myself to sleep when Dad left. I waited years for him to come back. But he's been gone for so long that I don't even know what he looks like anymore. He's gone. And I've accepted that."

Danny looked at me like he was disappointed in me, which I hated. "Finding him is not a good idea," he said softly. "Trust me. Him coming home isn't gonna change anything."

My mouth hung open, and I didn't know what to say for a few minutes. Finally, I said. "You're wrong. He could pay for your college. We just have to find him."

"You're gonna find Dad in one of the biggest cities in the world? Fat chance." Danny shook his head and looked at me like he felt sorry for me or something. "Grow up, kid."

I felt like I'd just been sucker punched.

"I'm sorry," Danny said. "Look, I didn't mean to sound so mean."

I didn't say anything. I was too mad to speak, so I just looked at the ground. Danny waited. He didn't seem like a powerful superhero anymore, like he did when he was out on the field. His shoulders deflated. I looked some more at the carpet, until Danny finally sighed and got up, his weight easing from the bed.

I guess my brother was kind of right. He always was. There were things that I knew Dad coming home wouldn't fix. Drew Balonik would never stop hating me. I would never stop being the last one picked for the softball team in gym class. Mom would never stop worrying about me.

But maybe if Dad was back in my life, things would be easier to bear. I could spend weekends with him. He could take me on his trips. I could see him work on his comics. Work *with* him, even—I had some pretty sweet ideas about how Gemma could take the nuclear superconductor back from the Raiders. Maybe, just maybe, he could even get a house on the other side of Sacramento and I could see him every weekend, just like Holly Berger with her dad. I could introduce him to Mr. Keanan. Man, my art teacher would love him.

What was he like, even? Maybe he imagined things in shades of colors like I did. Maybe he was also the kind of person who left colored pencils around and, you know, was okay with a little bit of a mess sometimes.

Maybe if Dad was around, I wouldn't be the oddball out anymore.

I forgot I was still clutching the comics in my hands. I sighed and leaned back. I turned on the lamp by my bed and looked at the cover.

When Gemma found her way to Planet X in *Spacebound,* she zoomed through the desert and flew through underground tunnels and barbed stalactites. Even when her spaceship was shot down, she still made her way to the cavern where her father was held.

I'd read that scene a million billion times, enough to

picture every detail now as I closed my eyes. Her father lifted his head; his face was thin and you could see his cheekbones. The room was dark, sketched in shades of rust and brown and black. Her father smiled. His twinkling eyes were the same as Gemma's and the exact same as mine, green flecked with brown.

"Gemma," he said in relief. "I knew you'd come find me."

CHAPTER FIFTEEN
RO

THE SATURDAY AFTER New Year's, I biked up to the launch site, the *Expedition II* strapped carefully to my backpack. I ran over what I had in my backpack again: the ignition, the timer, my notebook. This time, I hadn't just followed the steps. I'd tightened every bolt not once, but twice. I'd changed the shape of the fins to make the rocket more streamlined.

By now Benji knew what to do. He helped me set it up on the launch rod and then stepped back and brushed dirt off his hands. "Come on, smarty-pants," he said, grinning at me for encouragement. "You got this."

I hooked up the ignition wires with paper clips, and then pressed the button.

Ten. Nine. Eight.

I wouldn't look away, not even for a single millisecond.

Three.

Two.

One.

I watched as the *Expedition II* launched, soaring up, up, up, and my nerves faded away to excitement, because *this* time, it would climb to 1,620 feet. I frantically aimed the tracking device at the air, while listening hard for the radio signals.

This time, I didn't miss it.

I saw the moment it stopped accelerating in the sky, thirty seconds too soon, and careened off course. This time, I didn't miss the dead silence of the radio signals. This time, I didn't miss a second as the rocket teetered to the ground, a minute too soon and 800 feet short of the predictions. Better than last time. But still a failure.

Mr. Voltz held the rocket in his hands gingerly. "What happened?"

"I don't know," I said miserably, looking down at the patterns on the tablecloth. Ellie padded over, her collar bell jingling. I gave her a belly rub, which made me feel better. I knew that things maybe weren't supposed to go right the first time around, but we shouldn't have been *that* far off the mark. "Everything went wrong. The rocket barely launched before it crashed. The radio transmitter didn't work."

"Ah," Mr. Voltz said. "The radio I can help with." He

took a long look, turning the circuit boards and wires delicately in his hands. He pressed the switches and leaned close to the walkie-talkie. I sat back and looked around the house. I found myself looking at the picture of Mr. and Mrs. Voltz again. And then at the framed pictures of what looked like his kids, from years ago. Or grandkids, maybe? I couldn't tell. And to the far right, a worn baseball lay nestled in a plastic case, with a blue scribble on it.

Mr. Voltz straightened up. "These circuits just have to be rewired like this, and then you should be getting a radio signal. I'm not sure about the rocket, though. Maybe it's something with how it's built."

I examined it again. "Maybe I didn't screw on the nose cone tightly enough. Or the fins aren't the right shape."

Mr. Voltz shrugged. "Maybe. To be frank, I don't know much about rockets themselves." After a pause, he said, "You really built all this by yourself?"

"Well, the radio, yeah," I said. "But I didn't build the rocket all by myself. Benji helped me. And I had the fins and nose cone left over from a kit."

"Ah. I didn't know he liked building rockets, too."

"Well, it was a part of a deal we made, actually," I said. "Benji's supposed to help me build my rocket."

"And you're helping him look for his father."

I was surprised. "You know about that?"

"Benji told me. I've known his mother for a while. She took care of my wife back when she was sick." He sighed through his nose and looked down at the table. "I always knew that his father was . . . absent."

"Do you know what happened?"

He fixed me with his gaze. "Young lady, you know that's none of my business."

My face suddenly felt hot. "Right. Sorry."

The silence stretched out between us. Mr. Voltz kept looking at the table. I was probably supposed to go, anyway. But before I left, I looked up, back at the mantel above the TV. "Who's that baseball signed by?"

He glanced up. "Willie Mac."

I stared at him in disbelief. "Willie McCovey? From the Giants? No way."

"It was a birthday gift." I saw a hint of a smile. "You a Giants fan, too?"

"Yeah," I said. "My dad was. He went to high school and college in San Francisco. He used to take me to games all the time."

"Ah, I should have guessed. Your dad and I used to talk about them all the time." He nodded, almost looking uncomfortable. A long moment passed. Finally, he said, "I'm real sorry, you know. About your father."

I nodded, looking down.

"Does it ever get easier?" I blurted out. I looked back over at the picture of Mr. and Mrs. Voltz again. Mrs. Voltz looked happy. Like she'd forgotten there was a camera there because she was too busy looking up at him. "With missing someone?"

He leaned back in his chair.

"I thought it would," I said. "But I'm not so sure anymore. Does it ever hurt to even walk through the house, because you see so much of their stuff?" I swallowed and took a deep breath. "And you think that they'll come back, but then you realize it all over again that they're never coming back and your stomach starts hurting and you don't know how to make it stop?"

Slowly, Mr. Voltz took off his glasses and rubbed his face. He let out a long, heavy sigh. When he looked back up, his expression had changed. His eyes had softened. "Yes," he said. "Every day."

"He was supposed to work on this with me. We were supposed to build this rocket together," I said. But it wasn't just that; it was everything else we were supposed to do together. The birthdays and baseball games and drives at night. But I couldn't say anything else because my throat was feeling so tight.

Here's something Dad once taught me: the moon looks smooth from the Earth, but it isn't. Every time an asteroid or meteor collides with the moon, it leaves behind a permanent crater. There's barely any atmosphere on the moon, so nothing is erased.

I knew I could keep doing the Next Best Step. I knew

that when my world was knocked wildly off balance, when things were so beyond my control that I could barely comprehend it, I had to do the next thing that would push things a little closer back to normal. I knew I could try to cope with things by organizing the dish towels by color and letting Mom take care of her plants and play music on her record player. But sometimes Mom would stare off into space when Dad's favorite song would play, and I heard her crying in her room after Thanksgiving because she couldn't carve a turkey like Dad could. Sometimes I would be looking at the pieces of the rocket and I would feel this crushing pressure in my chest and a horrible feeling in my stomach, like it was being squeezed ten ways. Sometimes I couldn't help myself from wondering about That Night: how fast Dad had been going, what the force of the collision was, how much the other driver had accelerated. I could always do the Next Best Step, but sometimes I wondered if some people were meant to walk around with craters in their hearts for the rest of their lives.

"We were supposed to take a road trip across the country for her fifty-fifth birthday," Mr. Voltz said. "We were going to stop at every national park and ice cream parlor on the way."

"Ice cream?"

"Before doctors would tell us we were too old and couldn't have any," Mr. Voltz said. Finally, there it was. A small smile. His eyes twinkled. "She always liked to

130

have fun." He sighed. "Feels like a piece of you is missing, doesn't it?"

I nodded.

We were silent for a while, but it was the kind of silence where no one needed to say anything. It was a relief to be understood.

CHAPTER SIXTEEN
BENJI

I DIDN'T GET a letter from Amir this time. Instead I got a postcard, with a picture of Niagara Falls on the front. On the back, Amir had hastily scrawled:

Happy holidays! I'm sorry I haven't had the time to write lately, but I thought I'd send something over anyway. Hope your family is doing well.

I shoved the postcard under my pillow and didn't bother to write a reply.

"Ro invited you over for Chinese New Year dinner?" Mom had said dubiously when I first brought it up. She stirred the pasta in the pot and pushed her poufy bangs out of her face.

"I didn't know your friend was Chinese."

"Half."

Mom stared at me like she didn't understand. "What?"

"Like, her mom is Chinese and her dad is . . . you know. Not."

She took a minute to process that. "Oh," she said, stirring the pasta some more. "Huh. That's interesting." She covered the pot and wiped her hands. "So, what do people eat at Chinese New Year dinner? You should bring something, right?"

"No clue," I said. "I'm probably just going over to her house and eating some food." But as I walked up to Ro's house, with a plate of chocolate chip cookies that Mom had made from a bucket of cookie dough, I saw the warm light spilling out from the windows and voices chattering words I couldn't understand.

This wasn't just a dinner; it was a *big* dinner party.

But before I could change my mind, the door opened and Ro's mom practically waltzed out, with a spatula in hand. "Benji!" she said brightly, and then swept me up in a fierce hug. "Our very special guest."

I held out the plate as she shepherded me inside. "I brought cookies," I said. "Should I set them in the kitchen or—"

I stumbled into the dining room full of people, where promptly, three women turned and stared at me curiously.

Ro's mom didn't seem to notice. "I'll take them," she said, taking the plate from my hands. "Why don't you make yourself comfortable and I can introduce you to some of the—"

"I've got it, Mom," Ro said, coming down the stairs. I exhaled in relief.

"Hi, Aunties," she said, grinning brightly at the three women who, to be honest, looked like they'd never lost a staring contest in their lives. She turned me away. "Come on, let's go to the kitchen."

"So this is your family?" I whispered to her.

"Sure is," she said. "Those were my great-aunts. Laolao and Wai-Gong—my grandparents—are probably in the kitchen or something."

"They're all from around here?"

"Well, most of my mom's side of the family—the Lings—live in San Francisco. But everyone switches off hosting the dinner every year." She leaned in, lowering her voice. "Don't mind them staring. It's because you're the only white person in this room." She paused. "Well, one and a half, if you count me."

I realized that I couldn't see her dad anywhere.

Where was he?

Something sizzled and spat in the kitchen as it got dropped in the large round pan. A large plume of steam and smoke engulfed the pan.

Whoa. The aroma alone made my mouth water.

"Here." Ro pushed a plate at me. "We can start you off easy before we move on to the chicken feet."

Chicken feet?

"Kidding," Ro said, seeing the look on my face. "I wouldn't make you do that."

We found a quiet corner of the living room. Ro pointed to the things piled high on my plate. "Do you know what any of this is?"

I poked it with my fork. "Is this like bread or something?"

"You've never had Chinese food before, have you?" Catching the look on my face, she grinned. "I'll get to see you have your first char siu bao."

"The what?"

"This," Ro said, pointing to a round bun. "It's stuffed with barbecued pork. It's kind of sweet and smoky? Here, try it."

I bit into the hot bun, and my eyes widened. "Dis," I said with my mouth full, "isshogood."

I'd inhaled it before I knew it. Ro held up something that looked like those fried Oreos Mom would never let me eat at the fair, except it was perfectly spherical and covered with sesame seeds. "Try this sesame ball next."

The crispy shell crumbled into a sweet gooey bite.

This was *way* better than a fried Oreo.

"I can't believe you grew up on this stuff," I said.

"Sort of," Ro said. "We eat a lot of stir-fry. But my other grandparents come visit on Christmas and Thanksgiving, so sometimes I get a lot of shepherd's pie."

"You're so lucky," I said. "My mom burns the pasta sometimes."

She smiled and looked down. "I mean, I like it, I guess. But it's . . . definitely different."

"What is it like—" I couldn't put it in words. "Growing up like that?"

She sighed and looked out. "It's kind of hard to explain. It was weird when people would come up to my dad at stores and ask if I was adopted. Or when my Chinese grandma asks Mom if my freckles can be scrubbed off. Or when grandparents tell my other cousins that they look so much like their mom, or their dad, and I don't really look like either. Or when someone guesses I'm Mexican, or South American, or if they don't even bother to guess in the first place and just ask, 'What are you?' I feel like a freak."

She sighed again. "But they were so similar. That's the part no one understands. My mom and dad both liked the same rock bands. They used to go on road trips down the coast. They liked the same awful Italian restaurant. But just because they didn't look like each other, well . . . some people thought they didn't belong together."

Silence. *Used to.* Where *was* her dad, anyway?

Ro drew her knees up to under her chin. I wanted to tell her that she wasn't a freak. Or that it would be pretty sad if her freckles were scrubbed off, because they matched mine and because I couldn't imagine a Ro without freckles sprinkled across the bridge of her nose. I didn't even know

136

if my parents had ever gone on a road trip. Maybe they had. They probably hadn't. I wouldn't know.

"I didn't know that," I said. "I guess . . . it just wasn't something I thought about."

Ro shrugged. "Yeah, most people don't have to."

"You get these dinners, though," I said. "And this bun is the best thing I've ever had in my life." I looked up. "So what are these chicken feet you told me about?"

"Don't even try," Ro said.

"You know I eat all kinds of stuff."

She laughed. "You can go see for yourself."

We padded into the kitchen. The pantry door was ajar, and I heard Ro's mom talking to what sounded like . . . her grandma? One of the aunties? She spoke in clipped English. "I just worry about Ro."

"Ma—"

"*Aiyah*, you should move closer to us. More healthy. Chinese families grow up with their grandparents. And San Francisco's better than this place. You remember the Chus, right? They're still next door to us. Good support system."

"I can't," Ro's mom said. She sounded exhausted.

"I know this is a hard time for you," Ro's grandmother said. "He was a good husband. Your ba and I are sad, too. But we want to help. The Ling family stays together."

I turned to see Ro's face pale. She was frozen for a minute. And then she turned and ran.

"Ro!" I called, running after her, and the conversation

in the pantry stopped. "Ro!"

I found her outside on the patio, leaning against the wall. Her arms were crossed.

I stood by her for a few moments. The chill seeped in.

"Your dad," I said. "Did he leave too?"

She looked up. Finally, she said, in a small voice, "He was killed by a drunk driver."

I stopped. I exhaled. "Oh."

Neither of us said anything. I asked finally, "When?"

"Last March." Her voice sounded tight, like she was trying hard not to cry. "That's why I moved schools."

I paused.

"I'm sorry," I said. I didn't know what to say after that. My mind raced through all the things you're supposed to say after something sad happens to a friend. *I understand. I've been there.*

But the thing was, I didn't understand. I knew what it was like to have a dad who didn't show up for birthdays or baseball games. A dad who was generally absent on all fronts and could be in Nevada or Arizona or Greenland for all I knew, but I didn't know what it was like to have a dad who was there and then was *gone.*

Someone who would never, ever, ever come back.

And so I did the only thing I could do. I opened my arms for a hug, and she leaned her forehead on my shoulder. I kept not saying anything, but I guess she was okay with this. And then a couple minutes later I heard hiccuping sounds, and Ro pulled away and mumbled, "Sorry. I'm getting snot all over your sweatshirt."

"That's okay," I said. "I really am sorry about your dad."

"There's nothing I can do about it." Ro said. "About anything. My grandmother's been trying to push Mom to move to San Francisco because that's what everyone else thinks is best for us and they keep saying that I love the city. And I *do,* but I can't even think about moving. Because that would be like leaving Dad behind." Her voice rose. "And sometimes I can't help *thinking* about it, you know? That night. I try to figure out how fast the other driver was going and if he just slowed down a little bit more or turned more or something Dad might still be here, but he's gone and I can't do anything about it." She wiped her face with the sleeve of her windbreaker. "Sorry," she mumbled again.

"It's okay," I said. "I used to cry about my dad too."

She nodded and sighed. She leaned back, looking up. "He used to point those out to me," she said, pointing up to the inky sky. "Constellations. See, there's Orion." She traced a line. "That's his belt."

I peered closer and could make out three bright stars. "Did your dad like building rockets, too?"

"Yeah." She sighed. "We were supposed to work on it together."

And then my stomach grumbled. Ro looked over. "Still hungry?"

"Nah, I'm fine," I said, but Ro was already standing up.

"Okay, fine," I said. "You got any more of those pork buns lying around?"

"They run out pretty fast," she said. "Come on!"

And then we scrambled back to the warmth of the house, where Ro forced a smile at her grandmother as she scooped up two pork buns. We went outside again despite her grandma's protests that it was too cold. Because somehow, it was more comfortable out there. We heard the lone hooting of an owl and the rustling of the grass and all those sounds I usually didn't pay attention to because I never went outside just to look at stars. If I could sketch this moment, I'd mix dark against light blues. I'd blend in deep greens for the trees and dark gray for the shadows that stretched across the grass. We huddled in our sweaters and windbreakers, and Ro pointed out the constellations of a big bear and a small bear and what Ro said was supposed to be someone named Cassiopeia but I thought looked more like a flying squid instead. And so we stayed out there for a while, making up our own constellations, like the Intergalactic Octopus and the Massive Flying Saucer, the pork buns warming our hands and the universe in our ears.

CHAPTER SEVENTEEN
RO

"SO," MOM SAID, putting all the food into Tupperware boxes. After Benji left with as much food as he could carry on his bike ride home, after all our aunts and cousins had bundled into their cars and left, and after Laolao and Wai-Gong squeezed me tight and patted Mom and told her to call more, the house seemed so quiet I thought my voice would bounce off the walls. "Did you end up inviting our neighbor?"

"I did," I said. I'd invited both Mr. Voltz and Benji, but only Benji had shown up. I shrugged. Mr. Voltz had been coming over sometimes to help me out with my second rocket. He'd bring Ellie, who'd curl up in the corner, a safe distance away, and she'd watch us fiddle with the wires. He'd told me stories about how growing up on a farm in Illinois and hitchhiking his way to California before he went to fight in the war. He even made Mom laugh with his jokes. When he smiled, for once, he wasn't so scary.

I could see why Dad liked him.

"Maybe he doesn't like parties."

Mom shrugged. I sat at the dinner table, staring at Mom's back. I had to ask. I blurted out, "Are we moving to San Francisco?"

Mom straightened up. She turned around. "You eavesdropped on me?"

"I didn't mean to," I said. "Benji and I were in the kitchen. But are we?"

She deflated a little. "No, honey."

Whew.

"At least not yet." She pursed her lips. "But I'm really thinking about it, baobao. It might be good for us. We'd be closer to family. I loved growing up in the city."

My heart sank. I looked down at my shoes.

"It's just—" I looked around the walls. I looked at the living room carpet that had softened over the years, at the walls that Dad had painted yellow so it would look more sunny. I looked at Mom's porcelain vases on the mantel. I looked at the pencil marks on the door where we'd measured my height, in inches and centimeters, every year. We'd practically grown into this home. "I can't imagine living anywhere else."

"I know." Mom sighed and leaned against the counter. "We're just going to think about it for now, okay?"

My mind was spinning. Moving wouldn't just mean

leaving this house, I suddenly realized. It meant leaving *here*. Leaving school and Benji. Leaving the park across the street and the place where Dad always stopped to show me constellations. I felt dizzy, like everything was moving too fast, too soon.

Mom reached over to give my hand a reassuring squeeze. I didn't move. My arms stayed crossed. I didn't look up from the ground.

Just then, there was a faint knock at the door. Mom went to answer it. I glanced up.

"My kids visited me," Mr. Voltz said, out of breath. "They took me out to dinner, and it went on longer than I thought. I skipped dessert because I wanted to save room. Is it too late?"

He held out something in his hand with shaking fingers, and I realized that it was a hongbao, a red envelope, the kind Chinese families give to each other, filled with money, to wish each other luck and prosperity in the new year. "I wasn't sure what to put in here, to be frank," he said. "I got it on the way back."

So he'd wanted to come all along. I took his red envelope and grinned at him. I looked at the containers full of leftovers and Mom's eyes crinkled with her smile.

"No," she said, "you came just in time."

This time, I would make it right.

I'd taken the *Expedition II* apart and written down five

full pages of notes after the last launch. I'd described every single moment leading up to and after I pressed the button. I'd recalculated the math. I'd double-, triple-checked the radio wires. The numbers all checked out. It had to hit 1,620 feet.

Benji and I had already started working on the science fair poster board. Regionals were less than a month away. We had to make a perfect launch. I needed this. Benji needed this—he had to keep his art class. We needed our results, and we would get them. There was no way I could mess up now. I'd made sure of that. I'd recorded every single measurement I could.

This time, Benji didn't joke around as we set the rocket up on the stand and assembled the circuit. He just looked over and nodded, as if to say, *Ready?*

I stepped back and pressed the doorbell button. *1,620 feet*, I said to myself, over and over again, my tracking device clutched tightly in my hand.

With a hissing sound, the rocket shot into the air.

Please work.

Twenty seconds passed. It was still in the air.

Benji and I looked at each other at the same time, eyes wide. But there was no time to waste. I trained my tracking device on the rocket, my heart soaring a little.

The radio crackled to life.

Yes!

For a split second my heart rose. *This* was the time—

The rocket trembled and started falling.

The signals were coming through, but the rocket was already plummeting to the ground. The nose cone popped off, and the parachute shot out, and it was all over too soon.

We were silent for a moment. Then Benji asked, tentatively, "Was that a radio signal we heard?"

I nodded.

"So . . . we did it?"

I looked up at Benji. "Not quite," I said. "It reached nine hundred feet," I said. "It's supposed to reach sixteen hundred and twenty."

His eyebrows knitted in confusion. "But the rocket still *worked*, didn't it?"

I looked down and shook my head. This was the most frustrating part. When you were working on a math problem and the final numbers didn't come out right. When you got everything right until the very last step.

Benji let out an exasperated sigh. "I mean, this is *pretty* good, right? Isn't it good enough?"

He didn't understand. This wasn't like the Next Best Step. That was only for things that were completely out of my control. I'd *built* this rocket. I knew it in and out, calculated the numbers, attached the parts myself. I had to make it perfect.

Dad would have wanted it to be.

I looked up. "I think the fin wasn't secured on tightly

145

enough. I saw it wobble in the air. We have to do this again."

Benji just stared at me.

"One last time," I said. "We can't just end on this run. Something's missing, and the numbers aren't working out. We'll get it right next time."

He just nodded. "Okay. I hope it works."

"Me too." It had to.

CHAPTER EIGHTEEN
BENJI

IF RO'S GARAGE hadn't been a mad scientist's lab before, it sure was now. Because now Ro didn't just want to build any rocket: she wanted to build the most perfect rocket of all time. She was dead set on her numbers working out. We went straight to the garage, and Ro stayed there after I went home. She stared at her drawings and her tools for hours. If this had been a comic book, sparks would be practically flying from her goggles.

She even started falling asleep in class, and *I* had to be the one to poke her awake.

What had this world come to?

Ro Geraghty was going bonkers.

"This *has* to work," Ro said, right before we launched the *Expedition IV*. "We're on our second and last rocket motor, so we can't launch anything else. I triple-checked everything. I made the fins lighter. I even took out the bolts and glued everything down with extra-double-strength epoxy so it would weigh less." She looked up at me. "You're *positive* there's nothing else I could have forgotten?"

I nodded. "We just have to go for it."

Ro took a deep breath and pressed the doorbell button. I counted down silently. *Please, please work.*

Three. Two. One—

The *Expedition IV* launched straight up, trailing a clear line of smoke. Second by second, I clenched my fists tighter, waiting for any hint of a wobble. Nothing. The rocket cleared a clean arc through the sky. The walkie-talkie beeped steadily. Twenty seconds. Thirty, forty. It kept flying. My heart rose to my throat. And then—

The nose cone popped off, and the parachute billowed out.

I pumped my fist in the air. "Yes!"

Finally. There was not a single thing wrong with this launch.

I ran across the field to retrieve the rocket, unable to stop grinning. *Man*, I understood why people did this for fun now. I would have hugged this rocket if I could. "We did it!" I said, leaning over the parachute. I straightened up for a high five.

Ro's smile didn't reach her eyes. "What's wrong?" I asked.

"Nothing," she said.

"Something's bugging you," I said. "What is it?"

"Eleven hundred feet," she mumbled.

She couldn't be serious. I dropped my arms. "Ro, *come on.*"

"It was our last launch," she said. "And it only got to eleven hundred feet."

"So what if it doesn't get to sixteen hundred and fifteen—"

"Twenty!"

"Fine, twenty!" I pointed at the rocket. "Can we just forget about those numbers for a second? It went almost perfectly this time. The rocket launched exactly like it was supposed to! It didn't crash or anything. You even got your radio signals. Isn't that good enough?"

It seemed like it was good enough to get extra credit. At least, I hoped so.

"We can't just *forget* about the numbers," Ro burst out. "This is how high our rocket was supposed to fly."

Why couldn't she be happy with what she'd accomplished?

"Then what's enough for you?" I shot back. "What, are you going to launch a million rockets until one finally works? Why do we *have* to get this to this crazy height in the first place? You already built this all by yourself, Ro. You're a *rocket scientist.*"

What I meant to tell her was that she was a genius. That she was the smartest person I'd ever met in my entire life, and that included my math teacher and the kid down the block who moved away to become a spelling bee champ. I wanted to tell her that it was all okay.

What actually came out was: "Come on, it's just a stupid science fair project."

Ro looked up at me, and I instantly regretted every single word that had come out of my blabbing mouth.

Ro didn't say a word. She just stood up.

"Wait!" I said. "Hey, I didn't mean it like that. I—"

"No, you're right," she said, her words hard and bitter. "It's just a dumb project. Come on. Let's go."

We didn't say a single word to each other on the ride back.

CHAPTER NINETEEN
RO

IT'S JUST A *stupid science fair experiment.*

The wind tore through my hair and made my eyes smart. I could hear Benji faintly calling my name in the distance, but I just wanted to get home.

I rushed up to my door, but the door was locked. Mom was out. I fumbled with the key, my fingers shaking. I heard the screen door snap shut behind me. I raced to my room. I threw my rocket into the closet and then sank to the carpet, against my bed.

The Container of Dad's Things sat in my sock drawer, untouched. I'd never told Benji about it, I suddenly realized. I'd been so caught up in building the rocket itself that Benji never knew that I didn't just want to launch a rocket— I wanted to launch a rocket that would clear the sky and the stratosphere and go *out there*, into space and stars, carrying the picture of Mom and Dad. I wanted another *Voyager*. I wanted to build satellites and space shuttles.

How could I build anything close to that if I couldn't even get a homemade model rocket to launch right?

I glanced over to the corner of my living room, where the poster board lay against the wall, half-completed. The results section was still empty, waiting for our numbers.

Benji was right. This would never be more than some school project. We were running out of time.

I was supposed to have Dad's Levi's genes. His science genes. I saw the world the way he saw it: through numbers and reason. For every unknown there was supposed to be a perfect explanation. For every problem to be solved, there was supposed to be an exact solution, if only you did the steps right. Two chemicals put together in the right quantities always yielded the same reaction. Numbers weren't supposed to fail.

I had a Plan that I thought was foolproof. But I couldn't even reach anywhere near the predicted height.

I could never make a *Voyager*. And I wasn't a scientist: I was a failure.

I pushed through Mom's potted plants to get to the VCR. I took the recorded VHS tape of the *Columbia* carefully out of its sleeve, and then popped it in. Then I went to the fridge and took out some milk and made myself a bowl of Cocoa Puffs.

The cereal was stale, and I'd accidentally poured too

much milk, but the familiar chocolate sweetness comforted me, and so I ate it anyway.

I watched the *Columbia* rumble and tear into the atmosphere, like the very air itself had crackled and burst into a thousand tiny pieces.

I watched it ten more times, rewinding almost to the point of ruining the tape, and put my head in my knees.

I was supposed to be a scientist.

I reached into my backpack, pulled out my drawings and my diagrams and all the calculations I'd done. I wanted to rip them all to shreds, or stuff them in the closet. But that wasn't rational, so I stuffed them under the copy of the *New York Times* that Mom had.

I almost turned back to my Cocoa Puffs, but then something from the newspaper caught my eye.

Specifically, the entertainment section.

I scanned it quickly. And then I read it over three more times, not believing what I'd seen.

I sat straight up, and suddenly I couldn't move fast enough. I threw on my windbreaker and clutched the newspaper to my chest. Racing out, I barely remembered locking the door behind me before I was pedaling, fast and hard, to Hogan's.

It was there, right in the *Sacramento Bee*. I reached for another newspaper on the rack just to confirm. I stared at words and the times and locations, rubbing my eyes to make sure I wasn't reading it wrong. And then I felt it again.

The moment the cards turned and I figured it exactly out, and it wasn't like I was trying to guess or deduce anymore, because the answer was right in front of me, and I *knew*.

I knew where Benji's dad was going to be.

And I knew exactly how to find him.

CHAPTER TWENTY
BENJI

SOMEONE KNOCKED ON our door about a million times.

"Coming!" I shouted. What kind of mailman—

Ro stood on my front porch, out of breath and clutching a bunch of newspapers to her chest.

I definitely was not expecting this.

"Um, Ro?" I'd known better than to bother her after the rocket launch this afternoon, but here she was, turning up on my doorstep.

Her face was flushed as she pushed past me and came in. "We have to talk."

"Is everything okay?" I asked, following her to the living room. "Because I know you're still upset about your—"

She dropped the newspapers and turned around to face me. "I know how to find your dad."

My heart crashed into my rib cage.

She really *was* going nuts.

"Like"—I swallowed—"in New York?"

"No! I mean. I don't know. The thing is, I don't know where he lives, but that doesn't matter." She flipped to the entertainment section of the *San Francisco Chronicle*. "I know where he's going to be in a month."

I saw the part that was circled in Ro's bright blue Sharpie.

SPACEBOUND: COMING TO FILM SOON!

Captain Gemma Harris from the hit comic series is coming to life on the silver screen! Follow as she and her crew find their way home after a disastrous expedition, encounter friends and foes across galaxies, and get caught up in a mission that could save the fate of their home, planet Earth. Directed by Lawrence Fisher and written by the creator of the series, David Allen.

"Look at the premiere date," Ro said breathlessly. My eyes traveled down.

Premiering March 16 at the El Capitan Theatre, Los Angeles.

My mouth went dry. I read my dad's name, over and over again.

David Allen.

It couldn't be. I looked up. "Is this for real?"

Ro pushed the rest of the newspapers at me, the sections circled with blue Sharpie. Some had paragraphs. Other newspapers only had one sentence. But they all confirmed the same thing: The *Spacebound* movie was coming. To Los Angeles.

My dad was going to be in Los Angeles.

It couldn't be this easy. We'd practically *scoured* the atlas and phone books. I'd written him letter after letter. We'd hunted down and circled every single clue in his comics.

And yet none of it mattered in the end, because he'd be coming to Los Angeles.

In Southern California.

He was going to be in the same state as I was.

It would only take a day to get to him. Half a day, even.

"We could go see him," Ro said. "It's the day before the regional science fair. We can go early and catch him right before the premiere. And then we can be back by nighttime."

I looked up to meet Ro's eyes, and I swear, I could start imagining it.

Movie screens and billboards and glittering city lights. The lights dimming; the screen lighting up and becoming my world. The universe hurtling through the viewfinder of Gemma's spaceship. The first burst of color; the *whoosh* of Gemma's spacesuit; the *KAPOW* of explosions as each sound bubble and splash of color came to life. The roar of a spacecraft in my ears throwing me back, so loud I could feel the sound racing past my ears.

And my dad.

"Ro," I said. "You *absolute* genius."

And then I started laughing and I couldn't stop. Ro looked at me like I was crazy or something, but she couldn't help smiling a little bit, until that smile turned into a full-on grin. And then she was laughing, too, mostly in relief and sheer giddiness, until we couldn't stop and our stomachs hurt and our cheeks were sore.

We probably looked a little bit hysterical, to be honest.

But I didn't care a single bit, because we'd *done* it. We'd solved this puzzle. This impossible mystery quest. We'd succeeded in our mission. Against all odds, in this world of millions and billions of people, we'd finally found him.

I'd forgotten that after Captain Gemma Harris discovered where her father was, she actually had to find a way to get to where he was.

It wasn't easy. Not only did she have to escape captivity by the villains, but she had to resort to stealing one of their ships from the junkyard. And the ship's brakes blew out halfway through landing; luckily, though, she landed on a sand dune and got to her father's planet in one piece, maybe with some sand in her eye.

I didn't really have to steal a contraband spaceship and travel across the galaxy with bad brakes. But I had to get past Mom. And I didn't even know where to start with that.

How exactly does one convince their mom to drive six hours from the outskirts of Sacramento to Los Angeles so her son can see his long-absent dad? How does that kind of conversation go?

Hey, Mom. I know that you haven't seen Dad in a while, but he's going to be in LA premiering his Hollywood block-buster, so it would be really cool if we got to see him.

Or

Hey, Mom. It would be cool if you could give me a ride to LA. It's slightly farther than Danny's baseball practices, but I'm sure the view's gonna be great.

It would probably be easier to convince Mom to eat a spider. It didn't help that I wasn't that great at dropping hints, either.

"You know," I said as I toyed with my peas at dinner, "we could go to Los Angeles sometime. For a trip or something."

Danny shoved salmon into his mouth and gave me a weird look. Mom didn't even look up as she vigorously mashed up her peas with her fork. "I told you. We're going to Disneyland after Danny's graduation next year."

"But I was thinking that we could go . . . sooner. Like . . ." My throat was dry. "In two weeks?"

Mom finally looked up. "Do you know how much I make an hour?"

That shut me up real quick.

Meanwhile, we were done launching rockets. We'd used up the rocket motors, and we'd run out of time. But still, we had to put together our science presentation, even if we'd never gotten a perfect trial like Ro had wanted. As I added finishing touches to the poster board, she asked me, "Have you convinced her yet?"

In lunch: "Have you convinced her yet?"

At Hogan's: "Have you convinced her yet?"

"No," I said, once and then twice and then too many times to count. Each time, Ro's face fell a little bit.

She finally said, "I could come over and help talk to her, you know."

"Probably shouldn't," I mumbled.

"Fine," she said. "Look, I know it's hard. But think of how cool it would be to finally see your dad."

One night, when Mom was baking cookies, I finally cornered her. "I know where Dad is."

She didn't move. A long silence stretched before us.

Still bent over the pan, she said, "So?"

My heart dropped. I said softly, "I want to see him. He's going to be in Los Angeles in less than two weeks. He has a movie. He's *famous*, Mom."

She straightened up. Her expression contorted to a

deepened frown. She looked like she was in pain. "No."

"No? What—"

"I'm not taking you to see him. He walked out of our life nine years ago, and I don't want him to come back. Don't bring this up again."

"Mom. Come on."

"Benjamin." She closed her eyes.

"Okay."

Ro and I were finishing up our poster board in our science classroom when I told her. As she carefully glued down her diagrams and I drew tiny, intricate stars in the background to mimic a galaxy, I said, "So, Mom's not going to drive me to LA."

Ro paused, chewing on her lip. She was frustrated. She finally said, her voice sharp, "Do you want to see your dad or not? If *I* were you—"

"It's not that *easy*, okay?" I burst out. "You don't understand. Look, your parents actually liked each other. My mom hates my dad, and she's never, ever going to drive me there."

Ro didn't speak. It occurred to me that my voice had come out way harsher than I'd intended. "Sorry," I said.

"I was going to *suggest*," Ro said softly, looking hurt and playing with the sleeve of her shirt, "that we just go on our own."

I lifted my eyes up. "What?"

She looked steadily at me. She pulled a timetable from her folder. "We could take a bus, you and me. We would go down to Los Angeles and try to see him before the premiere starts. I can plan everything. We'd be back that night."

"Ro, that's *ridiculous*."

"Fine, I guess it is," she said curtly. "Never mind that. Then we go back to Plan A. We *have* to convince your mom to drive us down. There has to be a way. Right? Okay, let's talk through what you're going to say to her this time."

"*Stop.*" I was tired of being bugged about this. I puffed my cheeks and blew air out between my lips, sinking down in my seat. "I just don't want to think about this right now. Okay?"

Ro slammed her pencils down. She didn't say anything.

I looked up. "What, are you mad at me or something?"

She looked up, too, her eyes flashing. "I thought you *wanted* this." She jabbed at the newspapers next to us—the ones with any snippet of information about the *Spacebound* premiere. "I helped you get all this way to find him. But it seems like you don't care at all!"

"That's not true!" I shouted. Ro and I glared at each other for a minute, until I finally stood up and gathered up my pencils. "I have to go."

Why did it seem easier to escape as a hostage, steal an enemy spaceship, and fly across the galaxy? As I made my way to the art room, fuming, I tried to swallow the bitterness, but there was still that squeezing feeling around my stomach.

Mr. Keanan looked up when I barged in. He was surrounded by Coke bottle caps, arranging them on a canvas.

162

I didn't say a word as I made my way to my usual corner and sat down.

He cleared his throat. "Everything okay?"

I shook my head.

A pause. "You want to talk about it?"

I shook my head again.

He shrugged and went back to his bottle caps. "I got new felt-tipped markers today. Feel free to mess around."

That's why he was my favorite teacher. I hadn't been here for lunch in months, but he didn't ask any further questions. It was like the time when Drew and I stopped being friends and I started eating in the art room to avoid seeing him at lunch. Or like those weeks after Amir moved away, when I sat in the art room and Mr. Keanan let me mess around with his chalk pastels. All those times he never bugged me about anything I didn't want to talk about. He just let me sit and draw. And think.

The thing was, what Ro had said actually kind of made sense. She made lists in life and then she went down the list. Wasn't it just a set of tasks I had to do?

1. Convince Mom.
2. Drive to LA.
3. Surprise Dad.

Step 1 was taking longer than I thought.

But Ro didn't understand the silence in my house, the

163

quiet dinners. I looked at Ro and her mom, and I felt jealous, to be honest. I envied the way Ro's mom reached out to her and hugged her and ruffled her hair. I was jealous of the way she gave out smiles like a PEZ dispenser that would never run out.

I had been so close. Cripes, the movie premiere was less than two weeks away, and I *knew where he was*. But as I sat through another silent dinner with Mom and Danny that night, he might as well have been on Pluto.

CHAPTER TWENTY-ONE
RO

AS BENJI AND I stood in front of our class, our presentation board between us, it was just like the first day of school again. As if there were a line that split down the table.

We'd barely talked in the past week, since Benji had walked out of the science room after our fight. We still sat at lunch together, and he still shared his Red Vines with me, but we mostly ate in silence. I didn't go over to his house. He didn't come to mine. Even Mom asked if things were okay between us.

I guessed our deal was over. He'd helped me with my rocket; even if it failed and didn't launch as high as it was supposed to, we still got enough to scrape together a science fair presentation. Between the fin designs and the radio transmitter, there was plenty to talk about. I'd found a way to track down his dad. But still, it was weird to go home and have all this time to myself. I sat in front of my TV and watched *Doctor Who* with my bowl of Cocoa Puffs, but I couldn't sit still. I reorganized Mom's spice rack. I put the books in alphabetical order, again. I practiced my lines for the presentation and hoped Benji at least looked over his.

The thing was, we had been so close. We had *found him*. We had circled the exact location of the theater on the atlas, and I'd mapped out the roads and bus routes to take. Never mind that it was the day before the regional science fair—I was ready to help Benji meet his dad no matter what. But his mom wouldn't let him. And I wasn't particularly good at reading expressions, but even I knew, from the look on his face, that he didn't want to.

He'd chickened out.

If that were my dad—

I couldn't think of it like that.

"All right!" Mr. Devlin said brightly. "Scientists, the floor is yours. Remember: the regional science fair is this weekend, so I hope these practice presentations will help you get ready."

I held my index cards, which were getting constantly smudged from me shuffling them. As Benji opened up the project board, I felt a jumble of nerves at the pit of my stomach. This wasn't just my secret project anymore. *I* was going to tell the whole class about the rocket. My rocket.

Thirty faces stared back at me.

"The objective of our experiment was to test which

rocket design would achieve optimal flight," I said.

I started going through lines I'd practically memorized. But when I looked out at the class, they weren't listening. A couple of students leaned over and whispered at each other.

They were laughing and pointing. At me—no, not at me. At my project.

I looked over at Benji. He didn't say his lines. He just stared at our presentation board, his mouth open. I followed his line of sight, and my heart dropped into my gut.

Splashes of green paint—no, *slime*—were thrown all over the sides of the poster, over what used to be neatly printed diagrams. The bright green mess oozed down Benji's intricate drawings of stars and galaxies, down my carefully written steps and explanations.

I had to stop. But it was as if my mind had blanked, and now I was just blurting out the words I'd memorized.

". . . Fins were cut into three different shapes . . ."

I couldn't tear my eyes away from the poster.

"We measured the angle and acceleration of the launch . . ."

The slime wouldn't stop dripping.

"As scientists, we eventually hope to explore other planets," I rushed on breathlessly, not even going off the cards I'd carefully memorized. I could barely hear the words coming out of my mouth. I started talking faster, racing to get through the presentation before the slime covered everything. "Like the *Voyager* spacecrafts, which carried a golden disc of all human sounds to explain human life to extraterrestrial creatures—"

I kept looking at the drawing of the aliens, and my face became very, very hot. My ears burned.

And I barreled on.

"—Or like the space shuttle *Columbia*, which carried the first Spacelab to conduct experiments—"

"*Ro.* Time's up."

At the sound of Mr. Devlin's voice, I stopped talking.

The room was silent.

I was dimly aware of Benji beside me, with shock written all over his face.

"And guys," Mr. Devlin said, in a softer voice. "What *happened* to your poster?"

And all of a sudden, I couldn't speak.

I heard the boys in the back of the classroom snicker. Charlotte Wexler leaned her head and whispered to Holly.

"All right," he said, springing up out of his chair. He cracked his knuckles. He bounced on the balls of his feet. He cleared his throat. "Who did this?"

My face grew burning hot. I couldn't think.

"Come on," Mr. Devlin said. He cleared his throat again. "Did someone touch Ro and Benji's poster board?"

Silence.

"Class," he said, his voice rising in pitch.

And suddenly, it felt like the edges of the room were folding in on me. No one cared about the planets and galaxies and universes out there. No one cared about the exact angles and altitudes of rockets; no one cared that the slightest tweak in a fin design meant that the rocket could fly that much high higher or farther, that it might be the one to discover a new moon or planet or signs of life on Mars. There were nebulae and space dust and runaway stars and clouds of million-degree X-ray gas and No. One. Cared.

All they saw was the *stupid green slime*.

"I-it's okay," I forced out. My mouth was dry. "I'll just sit down."

"Well, great job, you two." Mr. Devlin cleared his throat nervously. "But we should probably, uh . . ." He gestured to the board, his cheeks turning pink. "Get that cleaned up a little bit."

The boys in the back of the classroom were doubled over, their shoulders heaving with silent laughter.

I opened my mouth, but not another sound came out. Slowly, Benji folded up our presentation board. I walked back to my seat. Behind my back, I could hear my name being whispered around.

I shrank down in my seat, tears pricking the corners of my eyes.

CHAPTER TWENTY-TWO
BENJI

AS RO KEPT on talking and talking and I looked out at the classroom and wished for the ground to swallow me up a little bit, I met Drew's eyes.

I knew.

He had completely, absolutely, 100 percent done this.

Drew widened his eyes, as if he were saying, *Who, me?*

But I'd caught the small satisfied smile when I first opened up the presentation board. When the others were giggling and whispering, Drew simply leaned back in his chair and stared straight back at me, as if daring me to say something.

He hadn't been scared of Ro, after all. He'd just been biding his time for the perfect awful prank.

Someone in the back of the classroom snickered. Tooth-pick was saying something, but I wasn't even paying attention to him. Instead I was looking over at Drew, who seemed to be one split second away from busting into uncontrollable laughter. I wished I had the Flash's shoes— I'd be racing out of this classroom in an instant, and then out of this school and far, far away. I wouldn't stop. I'd just keep running.

Instead, everything seemed to happen in slow motion as I folded up the ruined board and followed Ro back to our table.

I was *furious*. It wasn't just that Drew had messed up the drawings I'd worked hours on, even though I was plenty mad that he'd screwed up the one school project I actually cared about. It was that he'd done it to Ro, who'd seemed really excited to share her love of space with the class. And now, she was slumped over her end of the table, blinking back tears.

I'd thought I knew how to deal with bullies. I knew what Amir did every time Drew made fun of his accent. He would shrug, as if it didn't bother him. Drew never stopped making fun of the way he talked, but he never got the reaction he wanted, either.

Honestly, I could look away and not care about this. I could laugh this off, even if what I really wanted to do was to chuck the nasty slime right at Drew's face. This was just a seventh-grade science project, really. I could shrug and pretend this was all stupid anyway.

But I couldn't help feeling awful. Worse than awful.

Because deep down I knew that this was all my fault. It had been over a year since I'd ratted Drew out. Over a year since I landed Drew in detention and the Prank Wars ended and he started hating my guts. And over a year later, Ro was caught up in something she'd never been a part of in the first place.

CHAPTER TWENTY-THREE
RO

AS THE BELL rang, fury rose up in me. Red-hot, five-hundred-degrees-Fahrenheit kind of anger. I threw my things into my backpack, and as Drew Balonik slipped out, I went straight after him.

Benji stood up behind me. "Ro—"

It was Drew. It had to be. I'd pushed him down at the field and now he was getting back at me. I brushed Benji off and headed straight out the door. I pushed past people until I spotted Drew's floppy brown hair in the crowd and strode right up to him.

He turned. "Oh, hey."

I snapped, "What is your *problem*?"

He squared his shoulders. "What do you mean?"

Tears rose up, but I blinked them back furiously. "Why did you ruin it?"

Drew gave me that look again. That look of fake shock. "I don't know what you're talking about."

"You messed up our science fair project!"

"'You messed up our science fair project,'" Drew mocked in a high-pitched voice. "Come on, how do you know I did it? Where's your *evidence*?"

He was right. I knew it was him. I was 100 percent certain. But there was no way to prove it.

"I liked how you put your alien goo all over it," Drew said with a smug smile. "It was a nice touch. Made me actually interested in what you had to say for once."

I opened my mouth, but no sound came out.

It was *all over*. The science fair. My project. All because I'd talked back to him on a soccer field.

"I've never heard you talk so much," Drew said. "You should do it more. It's pretty funny to watch."

My eyes stung. I waited for Drew to say more, but he looked past me. I turned. Benji was standing behind me.

Had he been there the whole time?

"Oh, hey, there's your boyfriend," Drew taunted. "You know, people think you two make a nice freak couple. It's kinda cute, actually."

Benji didn't say anything. He didn't talk back to Drew. He didn't even look at me.

I finally blurted out, "He's not my—"

"Oh, sorry," Drew said, looking at his watch. "Don't

want to be late for my next class." Before he turned around, he grinned and said, "Good luck at the science fair."

And then Drew was gone in the crowd of people. And Benji was still standing there, completely silent.

CHAPTER TWENTY-FOUR
BENJI

AS SOON AS Drew left, it was as if my tongue untied itself. "Hey," I said. "Drew's a jerk. Don't listen to him."

But Ro stayed in place, her fists clenched, her back to me. And then she marched toward her locker without a single glance in my direction.

"Ro?" I followed her. "Hey, Ro, wait up! Can't you see—"

She stopped. When she finally spoke, her voice was small. "Why didn't you say anything?"

I swallowed. "Look—"

She whirled around. "You could have *said* something to him."

"You don't understand Drew Balonik."

"I think I understand *perfectly*," Ro said. "He's a bully. What else is there?"

But the thing was, she hadn't been friends with him before. She didn't understand that when you talked back to him, it was like inviting more trouble. She didn't understand that of all the times he teased Amir, he did it the least when Amir just ignored him. She didn't understand that Drew had done this because she'd stood up to him when he tried to ruin her rocket.

It wasn't like Drew didn't upset me. He made me sick. Every time he made fun of her, it was like my stomach would close up. But right now, a crowd of people were forming around us. I could practically hear the words *freak* and *boyfriend* getting passed around.

"It makes things worse when you talk back to him," I explained. Ro had to understand, didn't she? "Just let him say whatever stupid thing he wants to say."

Ro shook her head, like she was disgusted with me. And then she turned and opened her locker and her face turned pale.

The inside of Ro's locker—*all of it*—was covered in slime.

It dripped down the inside walls and into her backpack. Onto papers and textbooks and the number-two pencil packs she kept.

The people around us were talking, whispering to each other. A few giggled and pointed. I could see Ro clenching her fists, her shoulders tight. A few long seconds passed. When she turned back around to face me there were tears in her eyes and my heart caved in.

Oh no.

"Friends stand up for each other," Ro said.

I couldn't look her in the eye.

"And if you were my friend, you would have said something. But you're pretty awful at doing that."

"I'm sorry," I said softly, my throat tightening. "Are you calling me an awful friend? What kind of a friend bosses their friend around? What kind of friend talks during the entire presentation and doesn't let me speak a word?"

Ro said, "I—"

"It's always been about what you want!" I blurted out. Wait. What was I saying? This wasn't even related to what Drew did. I was supposed to be trying to comfort Ro. But I'd started, and I couldn't stop it. Everything I'd kept bottled up started spilling out. "I've just been doing what you want all this time. You're always doing everything your way. I don't have a say in *anything*." I glared at her. "I didn't want to be a part of all this, anyway. I only did science fair so I could keep my art class. But you wanted to build your stupid rocket *and* solve my stupid case so you could keep feeling all smart and everything. You never cared about what *I* thought."

Ro blinked and took a step back. I opened my mouth to say *anything* better, to take back my words. But the damage was done.

"I was helping *you*," she said, her eyes flashing. "I thought this was what you wanted."

178

I squeezed my eyes shut. What was *wrong* with me? But the thing was, I was mad. And not just at Drew—I was mad at Ro, too. Because finding my dad had always been a secret. *My* secret. But Ro had taken over, and now I felt so awful about this whole thing that I didn't even want to look at those comics anymore.

People were starting to stare. *Why were they staring?* I took two steps away from Ro. I just wanted to hide in the art room and do my own drawings and pretend this mess never happened.

Tell her you're sorry. Help her clean her mess up.

I said, "Well, maybe I don't want your help."

The silence stretched painfully between us.

Ro drew herself up. "Okay."

I didn't say anything.

She said, her voice quiet and uneven, "You're embarrassed by me."

"That's not true," I said. But I still couldn't look her in the eyes.

"You don't think I hear what people say about me? You don't think I know that they say I'm a homeless-looking, know-it-all freak?" Her voice rose. "What's wrong with me? What's wrong with wanting to figure out how fast the Earth rotates around the sun or wanting to launch a rocket because I want to know things? Because I actually *care*?"

All the air deflated out of my chest. "Ro."

"Call me a *freak*," she spat. "But at least I don't sit there

179

sleeping in class and drawing *flying cars* or *space musicians* or whatever stupid impossible thing you've dreamed up. At least I work like *crazy* for what I care about. At least I'm not scared of everything like *you* are."

I looked up. "I'm not—"

"I would have found him," Ro said, her voice shaking, tears in her eyes. "If I knew where my dad was, I would have found him that very day."

She turned to her locker and slammed it shut. Slime oozed out of the bottom, but she didn't seem to care. And then, without looking at me, she left.

I couldn't become invisible. I couldn't even fake a convincing-enough fever to ditch class and take a nap in the nurse's office. So I hid in the art room for lunch, which was pretty much the next best thing.

"You all right there, kid?" Mr. Keanan asked. For once, he looked actually worried.

I forced myself to nod.

"Okay. You want me to put something on? Music? *The Hitchhiker's Guide*?"

"Yes, please," I whispered.

I sighed and rooted around for my sketchbook. I pulled out the big folder I'd stuffed with everything the week before; the comics, the newspaper clippings and maps that Ro had told me to study. I took a long look at it and thought about tossing it in the recycling. I stuffed it back into my backpack.

At least I'm not scared of everything.

I clenched my jaw. Sure, I hid my drawings every time Mom came in my room. Sure, I'd given up on trying to see Dad, mostly because I couldn't convince Mom, but also a tiny bit because every time I thought about seeing my dad, my stomach did cartwheels.

But I wasn't scared. *Was I?*

I thought about earlier, when Drew was making fun of Ro and I just stood there, unable to speak. I thought about the look on Ro's face when she opened her locker. I thought about the slime dripping all over Ro's stuff and how everyone had looked on and stared, and I felt sick all over again.

I thought about the time when I'd seen the Pepsi explode all over Amir. I'd wished I could step in, be more like the superheroes I'd read about. I wish I'd swept in like Superman.

But this time, I had just stood there too. I hadn't done a single thing to help her.

I stared at my backpack. The day Ro had found out about the *Spacebound* premiere, she'd burst through my door, practically shaking with excitement. I remembered her wide grin and buried my head further in my hands.

Maybe she was pushy.

Maybe she liked to do things her way.

But she'd pulled every magazine and newspaper she could think of off the store rack that day, and I couldn't think of a single other person who would do the same.

Friends stand up for each other.

I had to fix this. I bolted out of my seat and mumbled something to Mr. Keanan about needing to get water. I raced through the hallways until I got to Ro's locker. The door was left ajar. I opened the door. I would clean out her locker. I could at least do that much.

The locker walls had already been scrubbed haphazardly, the slime scraped away. Ro must have come back and done it in a hurry after class had started.

And now I was even too late to fix this.

I slumped against her locker and put my head in my hands.

I was the absolute worst friend in the entire universe.

The bell rang for the next class.

People started trickling into the halls. I pushed myself up and headed back to the art room to get my stuff.

Drew Balonik rounded the corner just then.

Of course.

I looked away. But then something in me shifted, and I looked straight at him.

He stopped, as if taunting me. "What?"

I didn't say anything. I just kept glaring at him.

"Sorry about messing with your girl," Drew said, even though his tone told me that he wasn't actually sorry. Not an ounce.

I clenched my fists.

"You know, I think it's really nice how you take care of

these weirdos. Like you did with the Pakistani kid before he got deported—"

"Iranian," I muttered between my teeth. "And he wasn't deported, you idiot. He moved away."

"Whatever. I mean, it's kind of cute. And with new girl. Like I said, I think you guys make a good pair. If she stopped looking so scruffy all the time—"

I don't remember lunging forward or grabbing him by the shoulders. All I remembered was a dull clattering sound as I shoved him back against a locker. "Don't say that about my friend."

I'd just meant to give him a good push and walk away. But the next thing I knew, he shoved me back with twice the force, knocking me off balance, and then somehow my knees collapsed, and he landed on top of me, grabbing my shirt. I kicked out blindly to get away from him, hearing an *oof* as my foot nailed him in the stomach, and then as I scrambled up he grabbed for me again—

"Hey! HEY! WHAT IS GOING ON?"

The social studies teacher tore us apart.

"He started it!" Drew Balonik pointed at me.

But the people around us stared at each other doubtfully. The crowd cleared, and the principal marched toward us.

"She's not my girlfriend," I spat. "But she is my friend. And you don't talk about my friends like that."

"Enough," the principal said. "Detention. Wednesday to Friday lunches." She turned her gaze to me. "Both of you."

★ ★ ★

Three months ago, I, Benjamin Burns, would have been quaking in my shoes the moment I got a three-day detention. If not that, then surely the moment Mom received the call from the principal's office and got so mad she wouldn't stop talking while she was making dinner. "Ungrateful," she griped. "I tell you to do better in school, and then you go out looking for fights with that troublemaker friend of yours." She slammed down the casserole dish and shot me a look that could char the potatoes on my plate. "I can't *believe* it."

"He was making fun of my friend," I said quietly.

"Oh, and you couldn't think of a better way to deal with it than to try to knock his teeth out?"

Mom furiously signed the detention slip the principal had sent home with me. Danny didn't say anything, but when Mom's back was turned, he winked at me, as if to say, *It's going to be okay.*

Drew sat three seats behind me in detention. He leaned back in his chair, far enough that I actually thought the chair might fall out from under him. He twirled his pencil and looked like he owned the place. Which he probably did. He sure knew this classroom better than I did.

Why had I gotten myself into this mess? I could have just stuck to my brilliant original plan and avoided Drew for the rest of the year. But I wasn't thinking. I'd just *acted.*

I sat at my desk the first afternoon, angrily scribbling a

bunch of squiggles with my colored pencils. I considered making my math homework into a paper airplane. The teacher, Mrs. Nelson, suggested we read a book. Drew laughed out loud.

Mrs. Nelson looked irritated. "Got your signed slips?"

I reached deep into my backpack, scrounging through layers of comic books and folded scratch sheets of paper from math and a plastic bag of Red Vines, and pulled it out. The paper was crinkled, and Mrs. Nelson picked it up with two fingers like it was a smelly sock. She turned to Drew. "And you?"

"Left it at my dad's house," Drew said.

Wait a minute. Were his parents actually . . .

"Bring it tomorrow, then."

"Can't. Going to my mom's house tonight until Sunday. I'll bring it Monday." He'd said it as if it were no big deal at all.

I whirled around in my seat. Drew saw me looking at him and raised his eyebrows, as if to say, *What?* So the fighting hadn't stopped after all. His dad had finally moved out. His parents were separated. Divorced, maybe. And I hadn't known.

But how could I have? I hadn't had a friendly conversation with Drew since last year.

I was actually starting to feel sorry for him when I felt a sticky wad on the back of my head. Drew grinned from three seats down and lifted the straw to his lips again. I peeled the spitball from the back of my head and gritted my teeth. Mrs. Nelson was reading a magazine.

The second day, right as I was going back to room 204, a kid caught me in the hall.

"Hey," he said.

"Hey." It was Jimmy Katz, from my science class. He was the one who had gotten hit in the face with Drew's lunch Jell-O when our class was making Rube Goldberg machines. "I saw Drew putting slime on your poster. Or Ro's poster, whosever it was." He cleared his throat. "I wanted to tell Mr. Devlin, but Drew told me that he would put live crickets in my locker if I did." He wouldn't quite look me in the eyes.

I let out a sigh. "It's okay," I said. "I knew he did it anyway."

"Still, I should've said something. It's not right of him to do that. I felt real bad when everyone was laughing at you guys. I didn't think it was funny at all."

"Yeah," I said. "It wasn't."

"I'm kinda glad you stood up to him, though," he said. "Even if it got you in trouble." And then he met my eyes for a second and smiled a little bit before he turned and left.

I stumbled into lunch detention late. I caught three spitballs in my hair before Mrs. Nelson called it off.

I was so bored that I started going through my overstuffed folders, trying to find things to throw out. I finally got to the folder with all my comics things in it.

I flipped through it halfheartedly, at the parts circled in Ro's blue Sharpie.

The movie premiere had always been in the back of my mind. But now, the date was staring me in the face.

March sixteenth. As in, tomorrow.

I tossed the comics aside. Not that it mattered anyway, really.

But as the clock ticked its way to noon, I couldn't stop staring at the dates. I leafed carefully through the news clippings again.

At least I'm not scared of everything.

I picked up the map of California Ro had painstakingly copied onto a sheet of paper. My heart was racing. Something was forming in the back of my mind. An idea was starting to come together. And the thing was, no matter how much I tried *not* to think about it, I couldn't ignore it. An impossible idea—

Impossible things, Captain Gemma Harris, are often dares in disguise.

Volume 3, issue 2.

And it hit me. If I skipped this premiere, I might not ever see my dad again. Ever.

I looked at the premiere date again and again. I spent the rest of detention so hunched over my maps that I jumped when the bell rang. I peeled another three spitballs off the back of my neck.

There was just one more thing to do.

I stepped in front of Drew as he was about to leave. "Hey."

He scowled at me. "What do you want?"

"You don't know what it's like to be made the butt of a joke, do you?"

His eyebrows rose in confusion. "What are you talking about?"

"Well, I do." I didn't budge an inch. "It sucks, you know that? When you played that prank on me with the caramel onion and got everyone to laugh at me, I felt awful for the rest of the day. Did you know that when you ruined Amir's shirt, his parents thought it was his fault and punished him for a whole week? Or when you planted all those fake spiders all over Mrs. Campbell's desk, she wouldn't go near it until the next morning? Your pranks ruin someone's day. Or week. But you probably think that's hilarious."

Drew opened his mouth and closed it. He stepped back. "Okay, freako, let's not spaz out about—"

"You didn't just ruin Ro's day," I said. "You messed up her science fair project. You ruined something she cared about." Drew didn't move. I stared him straight in the eye. "I just wanted you to know."

And then I turned and left.

I didn't come back to the last detention.

CHAPTER TWENTY-FIVE
RO

IT'S HARD TO be alone, mathematically speaking. There were a total of six billion and counting people on the planet. In a room of at least twenty-three people, two people were bound to have the same birthdays. If it was that easy to match birthdays with someone, then surely it wasn't hard to find someone to talk to.

Still, I had never felt more alone at lunch than I did that Friday.

I didn't see the fight happen. But with those who had, the story seemed to change with every telling. Some people said that Drew was egging Benji on. Some people said that Benji threw the first punch. Some said Drew did. I overheard Liv Wallace in the locker room saying that she couldn't believe the quiet kid would throw the first punch.

"I heard he did it for Ro," Holly said. They stopped

talking right when I walked past them. Holly spritzed an extra big cloud of Strawberry Delight into the air.

Benji got in a fight for me?

At least I'm not scared of everything.

I'd regretted those words the instant I'd said them. I'd seen the hurt written across Benji's face.

I thought I'd been helping him all along, but maybe Benji was right. I thought he'd just kept quiet because he always agreed with me, but then it occurred to me that maybe *I'd* never asked him what he thought.

I thought that all it took was a well-crafted plan. For science fair. For finding Benji's dad. But now, neither of those things was going to happen. I didn't even know how to fix the poster board. Everything had fallen apart.

And worst of all, I'd lost Benji as a friend.

I picked bits of slime residue off my lunchbox. I hated this silence.

Was it too late to apologize?

It didn't matter. I was going to do it anyway.

"I just want everything to go back to normal," I said to Mr. Voltz that afternoon, leaning against the checkout counter. I'd come in here hoping to see Benji, but he hadn't come today. He hadn't been in class either. He was probably sick. I thought about bringing a Tupperware of Campbell's chicken soup over, just in case. I glanced over and straightened the comics. "We used to do everything together. Now lunch is just plain awful. What if Benji hated me all along? What if *I* was the only one who thought we were friends and I never realized?"

Mr. Voltz sighed, glancing at me over the rims of his glasses. "You're a good friend of his. I'm certain he doesn't hate you."

"He probably does now," I muttered. I'd thought that someone out there had finally understood me. Accepted me for who I was. I didn't even have to pretend to like things around him.

But now I'd lost the one true friend I'd made.

"What happened?"

I was just about to tell him everything—about the deal we made, about the rocket and how it failed to launch; about how we were trying to find Benji's dad through his comic books and how we'd thought he lived in New York but how he actually was going to be in Los Angeles—when the bell jangled and Benji's mom rushed into the store. She was still wearing her nurse's scrubs; her hair was piled on top of her head in a heaping frizz.

"Hi, Janet," Mr. Voltz said. "Is something wrong?"

"Benji," Mrs. Burns said, her voice shaking. "Have either of you seen him?"

Mr. Voltz and I glanced at each other.

"He hasn't come by in the past three days," Mr. Voltz said.

"He wasn't at school today," I said. "Why?"

There was a long pause. "Because Benji's missing."

Oh.

No.

Benji. Benji wasn't sick because he was home—he was *gone*.

My heart raced. Mrs. Burns kept talking for a minute more, but her words slipped through my brain in a fog.

Benji was *missing*.

"Benji was supposed to be in lunch detention today, but he wasn't. The principal's office called me this afternoon. He was supposed to come straight home because he's grounded," Mrs. Burns said, her voice high-pitched and panicked. "But he wasn't at home. What if he ran away? Or someone took him or something—"

"Janet," Mr. Voltz said, his voice steely calm. "Take deep breaths. We're going to figure this out."

"Maybe he's with Danny," I said. But there was an awful sinking feeling in my stomach.

"He's at baseball practice," she said. "I checked. Benji wasn't there."

It wasn't a coincidence. Today was Friday, March 16.

"I don't know what's gotten into him lately," Mrs. Burns. "He's been so strange. He used to just stay in and read comics, but now he's been getting into fights and—"

The Friday before the science fair.

The date of the movie premiere. In Los Angeles.

I reached for the newsstand and frantically grabbed a

copy of the *Sacramento Bee*, hoping wildly that I'd gotten the date wrong, that I'd somehow mistaken it in my mind. But suddenly, staring down at the newspaper, the words swam clear and the date jumped out at me.

Relief slammed into me—and then turned to dread.

I whirled around to face Benji's mother. "I know where Benji is."

And I knew that this was all my fault.

CHAPTER TWENTY-SIX
BENJI

I DON'T USUALLY pay attention in class, especially not on those career-fair days when everyone brings their parents and they try to convince you to grow up and be a doctor or car salesman or something. Usually Mom called me in sick on those days, mostly because she felt guilty that she always had to work and couldn't go to those days anyway.

But the one day I forgot to skip, I got to hear Liv Wallace's dad talk. Mr. Wallace wasn't one of those car-salesman people or those people who toted around briefcases and passed out pens with their company names on them. He was a geologist, and he got paid to go into rainforests and all these areas that hadn't been seen before and map them. He'd survived a snakebite. He'd once gotten scratched by a bear and gotten twenty-six stitches on his scalp. He told us he had a motorcycle, and he wore a T-shirt to class, and he told us to call him Ray.

I had to admit: he was actually pretty cool.

And Mr. Call-Me-Ray spent his half hour telling us about all the ways people used to navigate, back when there weren't atlases and maps and friendly strangers who would give you directions, because back then probably no one lived in your small corner of the world. He told us about how fishermen used to be able to predict a week's worth of weather and find their way home just by looking at the stars and at the position of the sun in the sky, even when they were far out at sea. He told us everything from how the Chinese accidentally invented the compass by rubbing a spoon to how the Inuit found their way home through snowstorms by looking at exactly how the wind had scattered the snow.

When Gemma barely escaped the planet that was holding her captive in the stolen enemy spaceship, one of the engine thrusters was broken. The dashboard navigation panel failed. She had to manipulate the magnets in her suit to help her find the planet that her father was imprisoned on. I even remembered the exact title and tagline of the issue.

A Mad Mission: Will Our Beloved Heroine Successfully Make Her Treacherous Journey across the Galaxy to Save Her Father?

Now, I settled back in my seat, the comic in my lap.

I thought about Gemma Harris crossing the universe with a broken navigator. I thought about people crossing these huge oceans to find their way back home with nothing to guide them but magnets between their hands. As the Greyhound vents sputtered out cold air above me and the bus jolted along the highway, I looked at the atlas with each road locked between the crisscrossing grids of latitude and longitude. Here was the entire world, recorded in tiny centimeters and millimeters, and I knew exactly where my dad would be. I looked at the circled dates and my father's face staring out at me and wondered how it had ever taken me so long to find my way back to him.

CHAPTER TWENTY-SEVEN
RO

"LOS ANGELES?" Mrs. Burns said in disbelief. "He could be anywhere right now, and you're saying that he's all the way in Los Angeles? He—he might as well be in another state!"

She had a point. Even Nevada was closer to Sacramento than Los Angeles.

This was all my fault.

I hadn't meant it. The moment I'd suggested going to Los Angeles by ourselves, I'd realized how impractical an idea that was. How were we supposed to pay for everything? What would we tell our moms? I'd just been so frustrated that Benji was so unwilling to go to the premiere, I was ready to throw out any idea.

But even in my wildest imagination, even when for a split second I'd thought of going to find his dad ourselves, it was always going to be Benji and me. *We* would go to Los Angeles. *We* would find his dad. If anything, I could read the maps and figure out where to go and time it so we'd arrive in time for the premiere.

And now Benji was going. Alone.

"He's not *in* Los Angeles right now," I said. "But he's going to be." I forced myself to meet her eyes. I tried to push the panic out of my mind. *I will do the Next Best Step.* Deep breaths, in and out. I had to be calm to explain this to her, so we could go to Los Angeles and get Benji as soon as possible. "He's going to see his dad. His dad has a movie premiere in Los Angeles, and Benji wanted to find him."

Mrs. Burns didn't move, but her expression changed.

She'd known after all.

Mrs. Burns's eyes flashed. "This is ridiculous."

No one said anything. I'd never heard the clock tick louder.

"Come to think of it," Mr. Voltz said quietly, "Benji did mention wanting to look for his father."

"I . . ." Mrs. Burns blinked. Her expression changed. Her face paled. "I remember now. He said something to me about this, but I never . . ." She swallowed. "I didn't think he was serious." She turned to Mr. Voltz. "What did Benji tell you about this? Why on *earth* is he doing this?"

"That's all he said," Mr. Voltz said. He let his shoulders drop. "I don't know any more about this, Janet. He didn't tell me anything else. I'm sorry."

Slowly, she turned to me. "*What* happened?"

"I . . ." I had to explain. From the very beginning.

I held up the copy of *Spacebound*. "These are Benji's favorite comics," I said. "And it turns out that his dad wrote them. Benji wanted to find him," I rushed on, trying to tell her everything even as the clock ticked on. I knew that every single second Benji was getting farther from us. "He never knew who his dad was and wanted to see him."

Her eyes narrowed and her lips pressed into a tight line.

"So I helped him find his dad," I said. I swallowed, my gut sinking. I reached into my backpack and pulled out the one remaining news clipping I had. Today's date jumped out at me. I pushed the clipping over to her. "And we came across this."

I hadn't just helped him. I'd dared him. I'd pushed and prodded him until he felt like he had no choice but to go. I'd gotten into a fight with him.

I'd made Benji go to Los Angeles.

This was all my fault.

"I didn't—" My voice was shaking and I fought back tears. "I thought he'd ask you to go with him. I didn't think he'd go by himself or run off like—"

I dragged in a shaky breath.

I made him do this.

I had to fix this. If I'd known something like this would happen, I would have apologized long ago. I would have talked things out with him.

199

But Benji was already gone.

Next Best Step. What was the Next Best Step?

"I know this is a stretch," I said, trying to keep my voice calm. "He must have taken the bus into Los Angeles to see his dad at his movie premiere."

We'd made plans, long before everything broke down, before Benji and I had stopped talking, before he'd gone missing. We were going to go to the movie premiere Friday and take the bus back to go to the science fair on Saturday.

But the science fair was the furthest thing from my mind right now. It was over. It had been over since the moment I saw the slime dripping down that poster. Now all I cared about was getting Benji back. I looked Mrs. Burns in the eye. "We have to go to Los Angeles," I said. "We have to find Benji at the movie premiere." I stood up. "Now."

She stared at me for what seemed like two hours. She put her head in her hands and rocked back and forth. "We can't right now. Not until we get all the facts."

My heart was racing. *What more did she want from me?* "Mrs. Burns, I'm a hundred percent sure—"

"I'm not," she said, her voice shaking. "What if he's not in Los Angeles? It's half a state away. What if he's still around here in Sacramento? What if he stopped on the way at some gas station and he's just waiting there? We have to talk to the police first. File a report. Search the area. We'll go to Los Angeles after all that's been done."

I clenched my fists. "But Benji is my friend—"

"And I am his mother." She stared me down. "I know how to handle this."

We have to go. That was the Next Best Step. *We have to go.* That was the only way to reach Benji. And yet his mother wasn't budging an inch. My breath was rising fast in my chest and everything felt dizzy.

Just as I contemplated racing out of the store and taking a Greyhound bus myself to find him, I felt a hand squeeze my shoulder.

"We'll go."

I looked up at Mr. Voltz in complete and utter relief.

"We'll split up," he said to Mrs. Burns. "It'll cover more ground. You go talk to the police and search the area. We'll go to Los Angeles, just in case he's there."

Mrs. Burns exhaled. She closed her eyes and nodded. "Okay. Let's do that. I'll have Danny wait by the phone."

"Will do." He turned to a lady who was organizing the shelves. "Marge, can you take over this shift for me? I have an emergency."

"Thank you . . . both." Mrs. Burns didn't look at me, and my heart constricted. After all, I'd gotten us into this mess.

Mrs. Burns took a couple breaths to steady herself, her palms flat on the register counter. And then she picked up her car keys and headed out the door.

I turned to Mr. Voltz. "Let's go."

"Wait," he said. "One condition." He handed me the

phone. "You have to make sure your mother is okay with this."

I grabbed their phone and dialed Mom. She picked up on the first ring.

"Mom," I said hurriedly. "I don't have a lot of time to explain this. But Benji went missing today."

I heard her sharp intake of breath.

"We know he's in Los Angeles," I hurried on. "So I'm going with Mr. Voltz to try to find him."

"*What?* To Los Angeles?" Her voice was sharp. "How do you know that? Did he say that?"

"We're *sure*," I insisted. "He's in Los Angeles, and we have to find—"

"No."

"What?"

"You can't go. Los Angeles is too far. I don't trust this."

"I'm going with Mr. Voltz," I said. "We're going to be fine, I promise."

I could hear her hesitating on the other end of the line.

"Please, Mom. He's my best friend. I have to help him."

"I'm coming with."

"What?"

"Listen, Ro. I have no idea what's going on, but if you're going all the way to Los Angeles, then I'm coming with you."

"You don't have to—"

"I'll be there. Don't leave without me."

And before I could say anything else, there was a *click* and she hung up the phone.

We raced along the highway. Mr. Voltz drove exactly ten miles per hour over the speed limit, clutching the steering wheel so tightly his knuckles turned white.

No one spoke a word. Mom sat in the passenger's seat with the map. She knew the way, mostly, because she and Dad had driven down to Los Angeles together in the past. I sat in the back seat, wringing my hands and trying to keep my thoughts from racing in circles.

How is this state so big? It was three hundred and seventy-three miles to Los Angeles. If we drove at exactly seventy-one miles per hour . . .

It would take just under five and a half hours. More, with traffic.

Each minute dripped by slower than the last. I was normally fine with silence—I preferred it, even—but this was the kind of silence that expanded and filled the car and pressed against my chest until it was hard to breathe. I stared at the unending highway roads. A sign appeared in front of us.

We're going to Los Angeles. We're going to the movie premiere. Benji's going to be there. We're going to bring him back.

I ran this plan over and over again and tried to keep

my thoughts from racing.

You did this to him. And what if he isn't in Los Angeles after all? What if—

I clenched my fists.

We're going to bring him back.

"You're out of gas," Mom said, breaking the silence.

Mr. Voltz glanced at the dashboard. "I'll take the next exit."

We pulled into a rest stop with nothing but a gas station and a Carl's Jr. We all clambered out of the car.

"We're near Bakersfield," Mom said, pointing to the map. She smoothed it down and placed her purse on it so it wouldn't blow away in the wind. "I'm going to get something to drink. Anyone want anything?"

We shook our heads.

Mr. Voltz pumped gas. I leaned against the trunk and looked out to my right, seeing miles and miles of farmland. The sun dipped into the horizon, turning the sky shades of orange and pink.

There was an audible *tsss* as the pump released. I glanced back. Mr. Voltz caught my expression. He straightened up and his expression softened. "Don't you worry, kid. We're going to find your friend."

I shook my head, my throat closing up. "It's all my fault. I made him do this."

Mr. Voltz paused. "No, you didn't. He did this himself."

"But I—" I started. "I was the one who gave him the

idea to find his father. I—" Tears welled up in my eyes. "I dared him. I told him he was too scared to. And now—"

What if Benji didn't come back? What if he wasn't in Los Angeles?

"We'll find him." Mr. Voltz's voice was calm.

"I just wanted him to find his dad so badly," I mumbled. My eyes smarted, and I looked at the ground to keep from crying.

Mr. Voltz didn't say anything for a second. And then he said, "You miss him."

"Yeah," I said. "I miss Benji. I want him to come back."

"No," he said. "Your dad."

I looked up at him.

He knew.

He knew that a tiny part of me, buried deep down, had yearned for Benji to find his dad because I wanted mine back. It was this part that wished, in an aching way, that getting my dad back was as easy—as possible—as putting a star over a city on a map and chasing it down winding roads until I finally saw him and everything was whole again.

CHAPTER TWENTY-EIGHT
BENJI

THERE'S A STORY my brother had to read for one of his classes in high school called *The Odyssey*. Apparently it was this super long and boring book about this ancient Greek hero who couldn't come home from war for twenty years, because along the way he kept running into inconvenient things like one-eyed giant monsters or wars or flesh-eating mermaids who sang songs to lure sailors to death.

There weren't monsters or flesh-eating mermaids, but as we passed miles and miles of endless flat land, this trip was starting to feel more and more like a twenty-year voyage.

Everyone on this bus was either sleeping or looking out the window, except for the teenager sitting across from me on the aisle, who was reading a book. A tattoo peeked out of his jean jacket collar. I tried to look out the window, but there wasn't much to see.

There were small towns with big gas stations and mountains in the distance.

There was an avocado stand.

There was a shiny red Corvette sitting by the side of the road that looked out of place.

We passed five Carl's Jrs.

But mostly there were just fields and trees and hills, and I wondered how much more farmland there was between here and Los Angeles.

Destination coming up in two hundred and twenty-eight cow sightings.

Amir was right, after all. A sea of cows really did come between me and my dad.

I sketched the Corvette. I traced out the sharp lines of the front bumper and lightly shaded it in. I drew the jean jacket–wearing teen in the front seat, his arm draped over the side door. I tried to draw his tattoos. I paused. Somehow it didn't seem finished.

I ate some chips and added rocket blasters to the back of the Corvette. The farmland outside the windows finally turned into mountains. We hurtled past highway signs and city names.

The outline of a city finally appeared on the horizon, with faint hills in the background. Hundreds of buildings rose up into jagged little peaks. The sky was beginning to turn pink, like cotton candy, almost. The pink was silhouetted against shades of blue. Man, if I could sketch the skyline with Mr. Keanan's watercolors, I would. I looked up and saw Los Angeles on the highway signs, and a thrill of excitement picked up within me.

It was finally happening. I turned beside me to tell Ro, forgetting for a second that she wasn't there.

For the first time I felt a twinge of guilt. What was I doing, going hundreds of miles to Los Angeles by myself? I hadn't told Ro about this. Or Mom.

I couldn't even imagine how worried Mom must be.

I closed my eyes and tried to stop worrying.

Just think of when you see him, Ro had said.

I tried to imagine that exact moment. It would be at one of those huge theaters with bright lights and velvet seats. There would be people dressed up in satin dresses and silk suits and a big marquee with *Spacebound* printed out in block letters. My dad would climb out of a limousine and onto a fancy red carpet. I would shout out his name and run toward him, and he'd turn to see me. I'd yell, *It's me, Benji,* and his eyes would widen first in shock and then in delight when he recognized me. The cameras would flash and the people would shout out his name, but he wouldn't care. He'd break into a goofy grin and I'd run down the red carpet and he'd crush me into a hug.

Really, it'd be like no time had passed between us at all.

The bus pulled up next to a big gray building and stopped. There was a big *tssss* as the doors opened. People stood up and yawned, stretching their arms over their heads. I stood up too fast and my head felt all dizzy.

Wait.

This wasn't the theater. It was just the bus station.

I had to get to the theater somehow.

Everyone was getting off. The bus driver gave me a strange look, and so I grabbed my backpack and hurried off before he could say anything.

What was supposed to happen now?

I walked around the station. I started to feel hungry again and thought about buying another bag of chips, but I only had twenty dollars of birthday money left and needed fifteen for the bus ride back home.

Okay. Calm down, Benji. Think.

What would Ro do?

She'd get a map.

A lady in a bright vest was sitting at the empty counter, chewing gum and flipping through a magazine. I walked up to the counter and took a map. It was filled with all these colorful tangled lines, and I stared at it until the lady finally looked up.

"You looking for something, sweetheart?"

"How do you get to the El Capitan Theatre?"

She stared at me for a moment and then took the map from my hands and circled a couple of places. "You walk to this bus station here. And then"—she pointed—"you get off here." She looked up. "Got it?"

I nodded.

Her eyes narrowed. "Where are your parents?"

I shrugged. "My dad's waiting for me."

Which was kinda sorta true.

I boarded a rickety bus. I hugged my backpack in my lap and held on to the map like it was a lifeline. I didn't even think about what it would be like to get lost in the city. I couldn't exactly walk back to Sacramento.

But I forgot about all that as the bus rounded the corner.

One by one, the buildings lit up with their bright neon red and blue and pink signs. Warm light spilled out of restaurants and shops. Music streamed out. Some car was playing Queen, the electric bass intro on full blast. There was a billboard for Taco Bell that was probably taller than a building. Another one for the new Indiana Jones movie with him leaping in midair, whip in hand. I imagined him racing through mazes and swinging from vines as he—

Tires screeched as a bright red convertible roared by, the people in the car laughing and whooping.

Cripes, this place was *neat*.

The bus stopped.

I got off and looked up.

And my heart practically dropped twenty feet.

I was facing the biggest marquee I'd ever seen. It was like some huge crown of lights or something, with a star on top and *SPACEBOUND: MISSION LAUNCH* across in huge letters.

This was the absolute stuff of dreams.

I checked the watch I'd borrowed from Danny. Six thirty.

Actresses wore big dresses and lots of flashy jewelry; the actors dressed up in suits and shoes shiny enough for me to see my wrinkled shirt in. Even in my Sunday best, I couldn't help but feel out of place. The red carpet was roped off, the cameras flashing. I ducked under the ropes, hoping no one noticed.

Seven o'clock.

My heart was about to beat right out of my chest. I didn't take my eyes off of the red carpet.

Seven fifteen. *Where was he?*

There was a swell of applause as the actress who played Gemma Harris stepped out. She grinned for the cameras.

Seven thirty.

People around me started whispering to each other as one last limo pulled up. A curly-haired man stepped out, and suddenly I just *knew*.

It was him.

David Allen Burns.

Cameras flashed. Photographers surged toward him, and I didn't even think—I just acted. I pushed into the photographers. Clambered over the ropes and right onto the red carpet.

He turned and—

"DAD!"

People stopped talking.

Cameras paused.

Approximately half of Los Angeles turned to stare at me. Including my father.

I was frozen. I had seen him. I had seen his face in the pictures Mom had kept stored away in cabinets. And yet—

It felt strange to be in front of him. For real. In person.

"Dad," I repeated, suddenly very aware of all the stares. My mind scrambled. What was I supposed to do? Or say? "It's me," I finally said. My voice came out small. I walked toward him.

He backed away. "Excuse me?"

Out of the corner of my eye, two security guards started making their way through the crowd.

"I'm Benji."

He stopped. His expression didn't change.

It wasn't supposed to be happening like this. He was supposed to recognize me. I stared at him fiercely, hoping to somehow make the wheels in his head turn. *Come on, come on.* I thought about saying something dramatic like *I've finally made it*, but the security guards were closing in, so I blurted out frantically, "It's your kid! Benji! Remember me? Remember Mom and Danny?"

His face went white.

"Benji," he said, like he was in a dream.

Finally.

"That's me," I said. I barreled on. I pulled my sketch-book out of my backpack and flipped through the pages. "I found you through your comics, Dad. I like drawing comics, too. You won't believe it, but it's the craziest story. I didn't know where you were, but then my friend Ro found you through the newspaper—"

The security guard had reached me.

"—and I took a Greyhound bus from Sacramento—"

"Mr. Allen." The security guard grabbed my arm. "We'll get this fan out of your way."

"I'm *not* a fan!" I shouted, and then security guard let go of me for a second.

A woman stepped up next to him. "Dave? Is everything all right?"

"Come on, Dad," I pleaded, feeling smaller and smaller by the second. He didn't move. "Don't you recognize me?"

The security guard tugged on my wrist. "Come on. This prank is over, and you're disrupting this event. Let me get you back to your parents."

I couldn't speak for a moment.

Prank?

"It's *not* a prank," I sputtered. Desperately, I reached into my backpack with my free hand and pulled out a folded sheet of paper. "Dad," I said, as a last effort. "Remember this?"

His own colored-pencil *Spacebound* sketch, signed and dated.

Some kind of recognition came back into his expression. He unfroze from his trance and came right up to me. The security guard backed away. My father's hair was slicked back with gel and was turning gray at the temples. He smelled like cologne.

But he was grinning at me.

He had hazel eyes, just like mine.

He squeezed my shoulder. "Benjamin," he said. "Of course I remember you."

Yes. Finally.

And then he would reach out and pull me into—

He backed away. "Listen," he said. "You can't be on this red carpet."

What?

"Okay," I said, because I didn't really know what else to say. Wasn't he going to invite me to watch the movie with him?

"Wait out here," he said. "Promise? Just stay put. I have no idea how on earth you got here, but I'll be out in a bit, and we can get this all sorted out. Okay?"

I nodded.

"I'll be out soon," he said. "Promise." And then he briskly turned. The woman said something to him and then he wrapped his arm around her waist. He shook his head and said something back.

Most of the cameras turned to follow them but some stayed on me. A flash nearly blinded me. I stumbled off the red carpet, and then turned to look back at my dad.

He was standing beside the woman, posing for pictures. They flashed smiles. I saw my dad take her hand and something on her finger glittered.

She wasn't just another actress.

I wanted to throw up. I felt dizzy and stumbled back. The crowd pressed against me and another camera flashed in my face. All at once, I realized three things:

1. I had just crashed a Hollywood movie premiere.
2. I was not going to see the *Spacebound* movie screening.
3. My dad was married to someone else.

I stared at bright red lights on the marquee in front of me. They'd seemed so welcoming before, but now they just made me feel sick. The air smelled like smoke and exhaust.

Back door. There had to be a back door to this thing. And then maybe I could sneak into the premiere—

I ran down the block, weaving through all the people. I circled around to what looked like the back of the building.

Doors. Lots of doors. I raced up the steps and yanked on the handles, hoping that the door would give.

They were all locked.

I slumped on the steps. The smell of the back alley almost made me want to puke.

And then it finally hit me.

I, Benjamin Burns, was a total and complete idiot.

I mean, what on *earth* was I doing here? I was half a state away from home and in the middle of a city that I knew nothing about. I stood up frantically and turned around. It all looked the same: the buildings and lit-up signs and billboards seemed to stretch on forever.

And how was there so much neon everywhere?

And Mom.

I crumpled back onto the bench, holding my head in my hands.

Oh no. How could I have done this to her? Mom would be worried sick right now. Sure, I'd left her a note, but who would ever expect their kid to run off like that?

But what if she didn't find the note?

What if she called the police?

What if she reported me missing and my face went on one of those lunchroom milk cartons? I would practically *die* of embarrassment.

I stood up, panic rising in my chest. That was it. I was going to back to Sacramento. I would take the next Greyhound bus right back before Mom had a nervous breakdown.

I rooted around in my backpack for my map. I pulled out my sketchbook and my drawing, but there was nothing else.

No map.

I saw a flash of a paper slip at the bottom. I dug it up and my heart dropped into my stomach.

It was the note I'd been meaning to leave for Mom. And

I'd forgotten to actually leave it for her.

If I were the Flash, I'd don my suit and sprint straight home. Faster than a hundred miles an hour. Faster than the speed of sound. I'd run from Los Angeles and never come back.

But here I was. With no superpowers. Not fighting villains or doing anything cool. In this bright and loud city, I faded right into the dusty exhaust smoke.

My mom didn't know where I was. *I* didn't even know where I was.

I was completely, totally lost.

I slung my backpack over my shoulder. I would figure something out. No matter what, I was going home.

I walked back in the direction of El Capitan. I saw its familiar marquee sign. A few photographers milled around the red carpet. I stopped for a moment, looking up at the letters.

Wait for me, he'd said.

When Gemma Harris had rescued her father, he'd pulled her into a hug and started weeping out of relief. But my own dad hadn't hugged me or pulled me in like he'd missed me for the past ten years. His eyes hadn't welled with tears. He hadn't lit up with a smile. He'd barely even looked me in the eye.

How could I have been so stupid? He'd gone off and gotten a new life, with his shiny suit and his limos and his cologne. He'd remarried. He'd probably forgotten all about

Danny and Mom and me.

My eyes began to smart. I took a deep breath and tried to ignore how tight my throat was feeling.

My dad didn't want me here.

I'd come all the way here and my dad didn't want me.

In first grade, my class was supposed to draw a family tree and write a sentence about each of our family members. I was so upset that I'd walked out of the class halfway through and hidden in the bathroom. Drew found me sitting on the steps at recess.

"He's gone forever," I said. "I'll never know who my dad is."

"He's not gone forever," Drew said. "Maybe he'll come back someday. Maybe he's just taking a long trip."

That's how I'd always been thinking of it since. Like it was just temporary. Or like it was a matter of time before I found him and he'd fit right back into my family again.

But maybe he had never been waiting for me to find him. Maybe when he walked out of our lives, he never wanted to come back.

He never wrote *Spacebound* for me. Gemma crossing the universe to find her father was never meant to be a sign. None of the comics were ever clues. They were just exciting stories that would keep readers up with a flashlight. Going on a quest to save your father from a booby-trapped cavern was just something exciting to watch in a movie.

I threw my sketchbook on the ground and stomped on

it. My vision started to get blurry. My drawings of Gemma Harris got ruined, but I didn't care, because I never wanted to look at them again.

Was I going crazy, or was someone saying my name?

Had my dad come back?

But when I looked up, I was alone.

"Benji!"

It was coming from the other side. Was it—

I whirled around—and then I saw *her.*

Ro.

CHAPTER TWENTY-NINE
RO

WE WERE ZERO miles from Los Angeles and we still couldn't find Benji.

We'd finally inched our way downtown through the traffic and made our way to the theater. We'd circled this block exactly four times, because all the parking spots were full and I wanted to keep my eyes on the theater just in case he appeared. Each time, the lights of El Capitan spun into view. We idled near the red carpet as long as we could, until the cars behind us honked furiously and we had to go. Each time, I craned my neck, trying to peer beyond the ropes and into the theater somehow.

Benji, where are you?

"When is this supposed to start?" Mr. Voltz asked. We were on round five, and the car was starting to rattle. "How do these events even work?"

"I don't know. Maybe that part's already over," I said. "But then he'd be in the theater for sure."

Mom turned. "And how would you know that, baobao?"

"The movie premiere's tonight."

"I *know* that the premiere's tonight," Mr. Voltz said gently. "But I also think there's a chance Benji's mother might have been right. What if Benji didn't end up at this—this premiere at all? I'd reckon there's a good chance he's still in Sacramento. Or let's say he got to this city. What if he got lost?"

I shook my head and put in in my hands. "We can't keep circling," Mom said. "We need to find a parking spot."

The car squealed around another corner. Slowly, we eased into an impossibly small spot.

We clambered out. I hurried toward the theater.

Los Angeles had seemed magnificent at first, with its twinkling lights and its endless buildings. But the streets seemed to stretch on forever. For the first time, I began to panic.

What if I was wrong?

What if Benji *had* gotten lost?

He could be anywhere in this city.

There were countless shops and restaurants crammed into each block. It would take thirty seconds to look through a restaurant. Five minutes per block. Multiply that by a hundred—no, two hundred—

I frantically scoured the buildings around me. This city stretched on for miles.

It wouldn't just take hours. It would take days. Weeks. Months.

Just as the panic was setting in, Mom stopped and pointed to the end of the street. "Wait a second," she said.

I turned.

I shouted, *"Benji!"*

I sprinted toward him, down the street and toward the doorway of the theater. Without thinking, I crushed him in a hug. When I pulled away, I saw that his face was pale.

Something was wrong. Benji was shivering.

Oh no.

"He wasn't there?" I whispered.

"He was," Benji said. His voice was flat. He stared at the ground. He stuffed his hands into his pockets. "I saw him."

"What happened?"

He still wouldn't meet my eyes.

Mom and Mr. Voltz were catching up with us. I tried again. "Benji?"

He snapped up. "I saw him. I finally got to see my dad. He was here at his red carpet. And then he told me to wait *out here.*" He gritted his teeth and shook his head, blinking furiously and looking like he was trying not to cry. His voice shrank. "He didn't even want to see me."

Mom sighed. "Oh, baobao. Honey. Come here." She reached for Benji and folded him in a hug.

He buried his face in her shoulder. His fists were balled up. "He didn't want me here."

Mr. Voltz wordlessly reached out and patted Benji on the shoulder. My heart plummeted into my stomach. I'd done this to him. It was my fault. Benji had come all the way down here alone, just for his dad to leave him again.

"Okay, that's it," Mom said, after a long silence. "It's all right. Everything's okay. We found you. We'll find a pay phone to give your mother a call, and then you'll come home with us."

We turned and headed down Hollywood Boulevard, silent and sullen. We didn't speak. Mom saw how upset I was and tried to put her arm around my shoulder to make me feel better. But nothing could make me feel better.

It was all over.

But just as we were about to turn the corner to the car, I heard footsteps pounding and someone shouting out, "Wait! Benji, wait!"

CHAPTER THIRTY
BENJI

MY DAD RAN out of the theater doors.

"Wait up!" he shouted. Cameras flashed as paparazzi followed him. He stopped dead in his tracks when he saw all of us, probably confused that I had somehow multiplied into four people: me, Ro, her mom, and Mr. Voltz. "Listen," he said breathlessly. "I'm sorry I took so long. If you want to talk now, let's talk." He checked his watch. "I might have to be somewhere at eleven, but—"

And then his lips were still moving, but I couldn't hear anything he was saying. My stomach turned over. Suddenly it was like I was seeing him in a new light, and now, I hated everything about my father. I hated how famous he was. I hated his movie-star smile and fancy suit and even fancier watch that he kept checking as if he hadn't just made me stand outside the theater for more than two hours. The long minutes had stretched into half an hour, and then an hour, and then after that I'd finally lost track of time.

I straightened up. "You know what?" Heat rose to my cheeks. "I don't want to waste your time. Go to your fancy party or whatever it is. I'm leaving." I picked up my sketchbook from the ground and threw it into my backpack.

"Wait! Benji, I thought you wanted to talk through everything."

"I *did*." I spun around. "And then I got kicked out of your premiere. You didn't even look at me twice and you made me stand out here, waiting for *forever*—"

"Look, I'm sorry about that. But maybe it wasn't the best idea to come in the middle of my premiere—"

"Well, maybe it wasn't the best idea to walk out on my mom and brother and me, either!"

My dad's expression froze. The camera shutters were furiously clicking away. Ro was behind me, and I could practically hear her jaw drop.

I absolutely, positively could not believe I'd just said that. But I wasn't going to take it back.

I straightened up, shaking a little. And then I picked up my backpack. "It was nice meeting you."

"Benji." His expression softened. He looked shaken. His hands dropped to his sides. "I'm so sorry. I really am. I know I must have been acting like a jerk tonight. And, well, in general. For the past nine years. But let me talk to you. Please. I want to explain everything to you. Even if it takes all night. It's the least I can do."

I stayed put. I looked back at Ro, her mom, and Mr. Voltz. Ro glared at my dad and glanced at me, and she gave the tiniest shrug, as if to say, *Up to you.*

A camera flashed.

"Look," my dad said. "Can we at least go somewhere more private?"

We ended up all going to a tiny diner a few blocks down, the kind that had grimy checkered tile floors and bright blue seats and tables with permanent ketchup stains. But my dad wanted to talk somewhere quiet, and at least the place wasn't crowded like every other café. On our way in Ro's mom stopped at a pay phone to tell my mom I was safe, and I felt awful. I walked with my dad, and Ro with her mom and Mr. Voltz. None of us talked.

I followed my dad to the booth in the corner. We sat. The booth chairs were deep, so the table came up to the middle of my chest. It made me feel like a kid. My dad insisted on getting me a shake and fries, even though I told him I wasn't hungry.

He cleared his throat and shifted in his seat. "So."

I stared down at my fries. I didn't want to look up. If I looked him in the eye, this would finally feel real and not like a strange dream.

But I did.

This was David Allen Burns. The artist behind my

favorite comic book series ever. I used to think that he was powerful. Invincible. I had built him up so much in my head, he might as well have been ten feet tall and wearing a cape or something. But under the bright lights, I could see the shadows under his eyes. His bow tie was crooked. Like Mom, he had wrinkles in the corners of his eyes. With his sleek suit, he looked out of place among all the bright aqua-blue fake-leather booths. He didn't look very much like a star, really. He just looked like any other middle-aged guy.

I wondered if I would look like that when I grew up.

He pushed a hand through his light, unruly hair. "I cut my *Spacebound* premiere short because I wanted to talk to you."

What was I supposed to do, give him a medal?

"Sorry." He closed his eyes. "I didn't mean to say it like that. What I meant was . . . thanks for coming, Benji."

I thought of what to say. Like, *Thanks for showing up.* You know, because he actually did show up after the premiere like he'd promised. But I could just as easily have said, *Thanks for not showing up for the past nine years*, and it would have been equally true.

So I just mumbled, "Sorry for crashing your movie."

"No, I'm glad you did," he said. "Really. And I'm sorry I reacted badly to it. I just . . . there were so many people, and I just forgot how to act." He smiled a little bit. "I guess you don't ever really expect your long-lost kid to turn up at your movie premiere."

Okay, he had a point.

"I guess I owe you an explanation. About why I've been away." This wasn't easy for him, I could tell. He fiddled with a packet of salt. "Your mom's probably going to tell you most of this. I don't know how much she's told you already."

"Nothing," I said. "Just that you left."

He winced.

"What happened?"

"Your mom and I . . . we used to disagree a lot, when you and Danny were little. On everything, really. And then I wanted to quit my job to become an artist. And I wanted to move to LA. But she wanted to stay in Sacramento, and she didn't like that I'd quit my job. And we were fighting so much so I just . . ." He exhaled. "Left, I guess."

"For nearly ten years."

"I handled everything badly," he said. "Your mom and I separated and I went to LA. At first I was such a mess and didn't have any money to support myself, let alone support you guys. I was looking for jobs. And your mom and I were still fighting. And then she told me not to call anymore. She moved and didn't give me her number, and then I couldn't call even if I wanted to. And it just seemed like you didn't need me in your lives anymore."

There was a knot in my stomach.

What, did he just think we'd forget about him? How could I? It was impossible to forget about him every time Mom set the table for three every holiday. Or every time people around me whispered *divorce* like it was a dirty word.

Or every time I went over to Amir's house for dinner and his whole family was around the table.

How many times had I imagined having a dad around? He would have taught me how to draw. He would have played Bob Dylan on the cassette player and left his desk messy. He would have gone to Danny's baseball games.

I said, "But I did need you."

"I'm so sorry, Benji." He leaned forward. "I want to fix this."

This was the moment. He'd reach across the table. He'd ask to come back into our lives and—

But I didn't know if that was what I even wanted anymore. I'd once imagined a hundred different ways my dad would come back. But I was angry now. I said sharply, "You married someone else."

He flinched. "I did," he said. "A year ago. Look, kid," he said gently. "Your mom and I aren't getting back together. You knew that, right?"

I nodded. Still, it stung more than I thought it would.

"But I've missed you guys. I think about you all the time, believe it or not. And I just want to be there for you and Danny."

I thought of what Danny had said to me before Christmas. *I used to cry myself to sleep every night. I waited years for him to come back.*

"If you missed us, you would have found a way to visit us," I said sharply. I looked up at him. "Do you even know how hard it was to track you down? But I did. I came all the way to Los Angeles, and you didn't even want to talk to me."

My dad shook his head. "I'm sorry," he said. He looked ashamed of himself. "I don't know what to say."

If I wanted to, I could have stood up and stomped out of this diner and away from my dad forever. I could have run over to where Ro and her mom and Mr. Voltz were sitting and asked to go and not look back. I could walk out of his life the way he walked out of mine.

My dad was never meant to be some hero or creative genius who left clues for me in his comics. He was just some guy who married my mom and then left us. That was all.

I glanced over at the other table and locked eyes with Ro for a split second before she looked down. I turned back. I took one deep breath. Then another.

He was my dad. And he was alive. He was here.

"You got a pen?" I asked.

He nodded and pulled a fountain pen from his pocket. I reached over for a napkin and wrote our phone number down.

"You can call me sometime," I said.

He grinned, relieved. "I'll do that."

"Promise?"

He reached his hand over the table and I shook it.

"Now spit on it to make it official."

He looked horrified.

"Kidding," I said. "Why does everyone fall for that?"

He leaned back. "Now tell me," he said, tucking the napkin in his pocket. "How exactly did you find me?"

I grinned. "Long story," I said. "But I found you through your comic books. I didn't even know that you'd written them. But then I found some artwork around the house that matched yours. And then I tried to look through your comic books for some clues because you weren't in the phone book. And then I thought you were in New York, but you weren't. And then I found out that your movie was premiering here." I shrugged. "Pretty simple, actually."

He laughed. "I didn't exactly make it easy to find me, did I? I mean, I live here in LA, but you made a decent guess. That's pretty good detective work."

"It wasn't all me," I admitted. "My friend Ro over there was the one who helped me figure a lot of it out. She found the newspaper article about your premiere." I looked over at the other table, where Ro was staring down, her head in her hands. I felt a twinge in my chest. "Actually . . ." I turned back to my dad. "Would it be all right if I talked to her for a bit?"

He took a deep breath and then relaxed his shoulders. "Sure thing, kiddo." He got up. "I'll get her. If you need me, I'll just be over there with . . ." He looked over at Mr. Voltz and Ro's mom, puzzled. "I take it those are your friend's parents?"

"Well, her mom. And then there's Mr. Voltz, the guy

Danny works for. He's real friendly, actually."

He nodded. "Got it." Before he stood, he scribbled something down on a napkin and handed it to me. "And that's my phone number if you need it. Call me anytime."

I gingerly folded the napkin and tucked it into my pocket. "I will."

CHAPTER THIRTY-ONE
RO

I SLID INTO the booth. "You wanted to talk to me?"

Benji nodded. "Yeah." But he just left it at that. He fiddled with his straw, not quite meeting my eyes. He looked at the table as if searching for words to say.

I wondered if we were going to let this silence stretch on, like if I just started counting in my head from one, I would count to infinity without us saying a word to each other.

One Mississippi, two Mississippi, three Mississippi, four—

"Okay—"

"I'm sorry," I said.

Benji looked up.

"I'm so sorry I made you do this," I burst out. "I never thought I was making you do something you didn't want to.

I just—" My words caught in my throat. "I just . . . wasn't thinking. Or listening. I feel awful about this."

Benji didn't say anything for a second. Then: "I wanted to."

That stopped me. "You did?"

"I was tired of not knowing who he was," he said. He glanced up. "You're right, you know. I was always too scared to do what I wanted. Like standing up for you to Drew. I should've said something after that science class."

I shook my head. "It doesn't matter now."

"Still does. Friends stand up for each other. And I was an awful friend." He folded a packet of salt and then unfolded it. He straightened up. "And I just finally wanted to *do* something. I was tired of being scared. I wanted to see my dad." He picked up his milkshake and shrugged. "I mean, it was kind of a disaster. I'd always imagined this whole thing where he'd spot me from far away and then I'd run to him and everything would be perfect." He shook his head. "But instead I made a fool of myself. Everyone was looking at me like I was crazy. I almost got into a fight with a security guard. And my dad . . . just looked confused." He paused and put his head in his hands. He mumbled, "And he's married to someone else."

I slumped back in my seat. "Oh."

"I'm glad it happened, though." Benji looked around the diner. "In a weird way. I'm glad I came all the way down to

234

see him, even if he was kind of a jerk about it. I didn't want to spend the rest of my life wondering what would have happened if I'd met him."

He went quiet for a moment. "Plus," he said. "It really could have been worse."

I looked at him. "How?"

"At least I got to meet my dad." A corner of his mouth curled up in a small grin. "Our plan worked."

I grabbed a couple of fries. "I guess that's true. At least you got here in one piece."

"I wasn't sure if I was going to make it back, though," Benji said. "I lost the map I had." He paused. "Oh, we might make the news tomorrow. For, you know, crashing a movie premiere."

"Benji!"

He laughed. "I'm sorry I got you all in this mess."

I shook my head. "This is all my fault."

Benji looked at me. "Hey, you're not taking all the blame for this."

"Okay, maybe ninety percent."

"Sixty."

"Eighty-five."

"Fine. Let's call it an even fifty-fifty."

I glanced up at him and smiled. "Deal."

He leaned back. "Hey," he said after a second. "Have you ever tried dipping fries in a milkshake?"

"A fry dipped in *what*?"

"I've heard it's actually pretty good." He glanced up at me. "Wanna try?"

I shook my head.

"Come on," he said. "You never turn down a science experiment."

I gave in. We each dipped a fry into his vanilla milkshake. "This actually isn't bad."

"See?" Benji took another fry. "Now let's try your strawberry shake."

"No way," I said, but curiosity got the better of me. I tried it. "Ugh!"

When I looked up, Benji was laughing. "You forgot that I'm willing to eat anything and everything." He turned the fry box to me. "Last one?"

I shook my head and smiled, and took the fry. I glanced up, meeting his laughing eyes, and knew that everything was somehow okay.

Benji shook his head, smiling. "I can't believe I *actually* came to Los Angeles." His eyes widened. "I mean, yesterday I was still sitting in that awful detention with Drew, you know? There was no way I was gonna come in a million years." He sighed. "Thanks for helping me find my dad. I know I was kinda difficult about it—"

"Believe it or not, I understand," I said. "I did tell you to run away across half of California."

"Yeah, but it ended up being worth it," he said. He

grinned a little. "I'm glad we made that deal of ours. And I know I wasn't the most helpful on the rocket, but—"

His expression froze.

"What?"

"What . . . date is it?"

"Friday."

"No, *date.*"

"March sixteenth."

Something dawned on him. "Science fair is on the seventeenth, isn't it?"

I paused. And then I nodded at the table, exhaling slowly. "Yeah. Yeah, it is." I looked up at him. "It's okay. I knew we're probably going to miss it, anyway. I mean, I gave up on it back when Drew ruined our poster board."

"You *knew*? You . . . were going to miss your science fair? For me?"

"I mean, of *course* I would. You're my best friend. I had to find you."

He stood up. "Wait, no. We're going. We have to get there."

"Science fair starts in less than twelve hours, Benji. It took us six and a half hours to get here. We're not going to make it."

"We *have to*," Benji said, putting his hands on the table. "We made a deal."

"Benji." I was going to tell him that it was okay. That it was okay giving up science fair because I'd found him, and that's what I wanted most. "The deal doesn't matter anymore. The board is ruined—"

"So we'll remake it." Benji didn't back down.

"We're . . . going to remake it? Are you for real?"

"A hundred percent serious," Benji said. "You helped me find my dad. I'm not letting you give up on your dream. Come on."

I paused for half a second before I said, "Okay."

We ran over to the table where Mr. Voltz, Benji's dad, and my mom were sitting.

"We have to leave now," Benji said. "Science fair starts tomorrow at ten o'clock."

My mom's eyes bugged out. Benji's dad checked his watch. "You're crazy, kid. It's eleven o'clock, and you're all the way in Los Angeles. You might as well get a hotel here and head up in the morning."

"We can't miss it." Benji turned toward my mom. "We have to drive up tonight. *Please.*"

If someone had asked me at the beginning of the year what the odds were of Benji practically begging to go to the science fair, I would have laughed and said zero without a moment's hesitation.

"Mom," I said. "The science fair really matters to us."

"You're going to make Mr. Voltz drive in the middle of the night?" Mom crossed her arms. I saw a hint of fear in her eyes, how her lips were pressed tightly together. "No way."

We all turned toward him.

Mr. Voltz gave Benji and me a hard look. His bushy eyebrows knitted together. He took a deep breath and exhaled. "This clearly means a lot to them. I'll do it. I'll drive."

"No," Mom said.

My heart sank.

She looked right at Benji. "First, I'm calling your mom and telling her we're heading back. And then we'll drive. In shifts." She grabbed her bag. "Come on. Let's go."

CHAPTER THIRTY-TWO
BENJI

WE HURTLED BACK toward Sacramento at exactly twelve miles per hour over the speed limit, with Mr. Voltz blasting music on the radio to stay awake. Ro's mom shrank back in her seat, clutching her map until her knuckles turned white. After she'd spoken to my mom, she didn't talk to us much. She'd just told us she wanted us to get home as soon as possible. "I told her I'd get you back by the morning," she said to me. "And then you might have some explaining to do."

I'd nodded, my heart sinking.

But right now, on the way home, I tried to calm myself down. I hummed along and drummed my fingers a little. During the guitar solo I leaned toward Ro. "This guy," I said, "is *way* cooler than I thought he was."

"I heard that," Mr. Voltz said.

She simply nodded and stared out the window.

I leaned over. "Everything okay?"

"It's just," she said. "This is crazy, Benji. We're totally unprepared for tomorrow. We haven't rehearsed. And the thing is, the rocket failed. I thought I had it all figured out, how high it was supposed to reach and how far it was supposed to fly. And none of that happened." She looked at me. "How am I ever supposed to build a real rocket if I can't even build one for the science fair?" She put her head in her hands.

I sighed. "It's okay," I said. "Nothing that we planned really turned out like we wanted it to."

She glanced up. "You can say that again."

"I mean, I went all the way down there to reunite with my dad, and all I did was crash a Hollywood movie premiere. You know what? It was so bad that the security guards thought it was a prank."

She laughed. "Hey, I'm still proud of you."

"I know. I couldn't have made a bigger fool of myself if I tried."

"Not that," she said. "You finally got to see your dad."

"Yeah," I said. "I guess I did." I glanced at her. "And you built a rocket. That's still really cool. We both had big plans, and we both pulled them off. Mostly."

She nodded. "I guess sometimes there are just things we don't really account for."

I leaned back. *I guess so.* "Okay," I said. "What's next, then?"

Ro glanced at me. For a moment her eyes were still wide with excitement, but then her shoulders deflated a little. She leaned back against the headrest. "We really have to redo it, don't we? There's no way we can fix it, is there? I mean the poster we had . . ."

Was buried under a heap of slime goo, thanks to Drew.

"Yeah," I said softly. "I guess there's no other way."

"And we took *weeks* to make that poster, Benji. And now we have"—she glanced at her watch—"Around five hours once we get home. I mean, is it even possible?"

We were both quiet for a moment. I glanced up and met Mr. Voltz's eyes in the rearview mirror. He raised his caterpillar eyebrows and, so subtly I almost missed it, gave me a little nod.

It was going to happen. *We* were going to make it happen. "Listen, you're friends with someone who still thinks aliens are real, used to think that people had secret superpowers, and just ran away across practically half of California. Not that I would recommend the last part. But after all this, anything is possible, really." I leaned forward. "We're gonna make the science fair. I promise. We just need a plan."

A small smile slowly crept into Ro's expression. "Benji Burns with a plan?"

I grinned. "Looks like you've rubbed off on me after all."

She sat up. "You want to remake the poster board when we get home? For real?"

I nodded. "A million percent."

Ro's mom glanced at us. "Benji, not you. You can't be remaking the poster board."

"But Mom, our poster board was ruined. He has to help—"

"Enough. Ro, he's in enough trouble as is. Do you know how scary it is when your own kid goes missing for a day? I *promised* his mother I'd get him home—"

"By the *morning*," I said. "Please, Mrs. Geraghty. I have to do this. We've worked so hard on this, and we're really proud of what we've done. We need to make the science fair."

Ro's mom stared at us.

A million seconds seemed to pass.

"Well," she said, very quietly. "I did tell her it might take all night to drive you back, given how long it took for us to get to LA." She paused. "But we seem to be moving faster than we were before."

"Much faster," Mr. Voltz added, his eyes trained on the road. "There's practically no traffic out here. We might even be home by four thirty."

Ro's mom was silent for a while. Finally she looked up. "You may stay at our house to finish your science fair poster. But the *instant* the sun rises, I am taking you home. Understood?"

Ro and I nodded. She grinned and turned to me. "Okay, I still have all the numbers in my notebook, so it shouldn't be hard to copy them down. We might have to rewrite parts of the poster, but I've got the drafts in my folder. We have some leftover cardboard for the poster board, and some of the construction paper to cover it." She turned to me. "You think you can replicate your drawings?"

Her eyes had lit up. I could practically *see* her mind working furiously to make it all come together, break it down to a perfectly written step-by-step list, and make the impossible possible again. I smiled. "Absolutely."

The science fair was back on.

CHAPTER THIRTY-THREE
RO

BENJI AND I hadn't spoken all week, but once we were back, it was like no time had passed between us.

Mom had turned to Benji the moment we walked through the door. "You have until morning to work on this poster, and then I'm sending you home."

We raced through the dawn. Benji grabbed the markers and set to work on re-creating his drawings. I cranked up the radio to keep us awake. Mom brewed us some of her extra-strong jasmine green tea. The rocket had been sitting in the corner of my garage, collecting dust. I polished it off, set it on its stand, and started copying down the figures.

I was through my second cup of green tea and still copying down my calculations when I leaned back.

Something didn't look right, and I couldn't quite figure out exactly what it was.

Wait a minute.

I thought about what I'd said to Benji on the car ride home, about things we don't account for. It was almost as if something was sticking at the back of my mind. Something was missing. I knew it.

I clapped my hands over my ears to block out the loud music so I could think better. I squeezed my eyes shut. *Things we don't account for . . .*

"Ro?" Benji asked.

"I'm okay," I said. "Just thinking."

I tried to think back to the rocket launches. I pictured us setting up the rocket on the launchpad. Pressing the ignition button. Watching as the rocket hurtled up for a thrilling few seconds, and then slowed its ascent, until it finally coasted and the parachute deployed. I felt Benji tapping my shoulder, but I squeezed my eyes tighter, imagining the rocket wobbling on its descent, buffeted by the wind—

Wind resistance.

That's it.

I yanked my hands away from my ears.

That's what we forgot to calculate.

"Are you okay?" Benji asked. "You have this crazy look on your face."

"Hold on." I redrew the entire diagram of the rocket. I rewrote every equation, jotting down the approximate numbers my dad and I had used. I went line by line and recalculated everything, until I finally reached the final answer and leaned back with a sigh of relief.

It all made sense, *finally*.

It finally all added up.

I grinned and turned to Benji. "Only seventy feet," I said.

"What?"

"We weren't hundreds of feet off," I said, pointing to the numbers. "I forgot to count the wind resistance that would slow the rocket down. The final rocket launch was only seventy feet off."

His eyes widened. "Does that mean—"

"We did it," I said, almost laughing from the sheer relief. We had been working on this for months and months, racking our brains, only to have finally figured it out while redoing the poster board, with Dad's favorite rock music on full blast and just hours to spare before the science fair. "Our rocket didn't fail after all."

"Ro! Get up, baobao."

Mom was standing over me.

"It's nine thirty. We have to go. Science fair starts at ten."

I jolted awake. For a moment I looked around wildly. What day was it? And what time?

Science fair. Benji.

I leapt to my feet. "Benji—"

"Is going to meet you there," Mom said. "I drove him

home just two hours ago. Talked to his mom for a little bit. She'd been worried sick."

It was all coming back to me. Benji and I frantically reworking the equations and the conclusion to include the wind resistance. Benji putting the finishing touches on the new poster and poking me awake. By the time we were done, it was nearly seven in the morning.

My heart raced. But what if his mom was so mad she didn't let him come to science fair? What if—

There was no use thinking about it now.

I got dressed in two minutes and took another to rummage through the pantry until I found the box of strawberry Pop-Tarts. Mom didn't even change—she just drove me in her robe and slippers, her hair up in a bun. She drove at exactly seven miles per hour above the speed limit. I held our poster board the entire time.

We screeched up to the parking lot of the high school hosting the regional science fair. Mom leaned over the passenger's seat to give me a kiss. "Pick you up at three?"

I nodded.

"Good luck, baobao."

I sprinted into the school, clutching the poster board awkwardly to my chest.

It was the biggest gym I'd ever seen, with high ceilings and shiny wood floors and lights so bright they were disorienting. Rows and rows of tables were lined with colorful posters. There were projects on everything from earthworms to lemon-powered clocks. I checked the time on my watch and looked around frantically.

It was 9:50.

The schools had to be in alphabetical order. *Carmichael, Hoover, Lowell—*

"Ro!"

Mr. Devlin hurried down the row. He was wearing his smiley-face tie today, but his face was all red and he looked flustered. "Where have you been? You were supposed to be here half an hour ago! We're nowhere near ready."

Oh no. Did Benji also—

He was standing at the edge of the table, dressed up in a shirt and tie. He grinned when he saw me.

"Ro Geraghty, finally late to something?"

"Overslept," I muttered.

"Okay, listen," Mr. Devlin said. I could see his eye start to twitch. He started circling things on his clipboard. "We're running behind." He glanced at me. "And that is—?"

"The new poster board," I said. "Since our old one got ruined. And it has some new info on it, too."

Mr. Devlin stared at us. "But your poster board was cleaned up this week. Did you not—?" He pulled it up and opened it. "I mean, that's why I thought you guys were still coming today."

I glanced over at the old poster board.

It was spotless. Well, almost. I could still see a tiny bit of green slime at the bottom right corner, but all the rest of the slime was gone. The parts of the poster that had been covered were carefully colored over, so that it matched the surroundings. The graphs that were once ruined had been carefully traced and redone.

It was as if nothing had happened.

It was incredible.

Benji and I looked at each other. "Did you—"

"Nope."

"Wasn't me," he said.

I turned to Mr. Devlin. "I think we're still going with this new poster board. We updated our results a little."

His brow furrowed. "Are you sure? I'm a little worried about this new material, since we didn't rehearse—"

"We'll be *fine*, Mr. Devlin," I said.

He looked up in surprise.

"I promise," I said.

He nodded. "Just don't forget to introduce yourselves," he said. Just then, someone called his name and he hurried over, but not before giving us a big thumbs-up.

Benji glanced at the cleaned-up poster in disbelief and then looked at me. But we didn't have time to figure out what had happened, because right then the clock ticked to ten. And the old poster didn't matter anymore—we had our new poster. With the carefully recopied charts and the rewritten equations, with numbers that worked out. With Benji's drawings of spinning galaxies and clouds of spacedust.

I set the new poster up and placed the rocket on the stand.

Judges made their way over to us.

Benji turned to me and grinned.

T minus zero.

I turned and took a deep breath. I smiled. "I'm Ro Geraghty and this is Benji Burns. In our science experiment, we tested the effect of a rocket's structural changes on its flight path."

I led them through each re-pasted picture and each graph. Benji nailed his lines. We were halfway through our presentation when I realized: They didn't know that I'd once thought my science experiment was a failure. They didn't know that just a few days ago, we had a faulty presentation board that was dripping with slime. They didn't know that last night, we were in the middle of Los Angeles and weren't even sure if we'd make it here. They didn't know that everything fell into place just a few hours ago.

Instead, this is what they saw: a carefully built science fair project. Meticulously constructed model rockets. Rocket launches that had shaky starts but ultimately landed one last successful trial.

I thought about eating Cocoa Puffs in front of the TV with Dad, watching the *Columbia* launch. I thought about Dad telling me about each of the space launches he'd seen as a kid, the ones that started with just sending a steel box into

251

space and then got more and more elaborate until he finally saw Neil Armstrong step on the moon.

Those were just the successes. But how many failures did the scientists have to see? How many times did their rockets not orbit the planet, or not take off at all? How many times had they dreamed about landing on the moon, only to realize that they couldn't make it happen, not yet?

Scientists are detectives. They go into deep oceans and to the ends of thick jungles to find the clues to the universe. They stare at things under a microscope and crane their necks at the stars, always hoping to find something new.

But scientists are also detectives who go on missions that don't work. Who climb to the edges of jungles that yield nothing. Who hunch over a microscope looking at things that don't make sense. Who stare at the universe and recalculate the entire system of gravity and space and time until everything finally matches up. Sometimes, science means looking at the cards ten times before you finally catch the trick. It means failing, and trying, and failing again, all in hopes of making things better the next time around.

CHAPTER THIRTY-FOUR
BENJI

WE ACED IT.

Ro didn't stumble one bit. She talked like she'd known this stuff for her entire life, which probably wasn't much of an exaggeration. Over and over again, as different judges wandered over, Ro explained the angles and the settings of the rockets, and I explained the graphs. At some point, more and more judges kept coming over to our poster, until there was a small crowd around our table. Every time someone asked us a question, her face lit up. The judges practically spent *hours* looking over her radio transmission system, saying they'd never seen middle schoolers with the likes of this project.

Get this: I *liked* talking. My face and hands didn't turn all red and itchy like they used to. My words didn't close up before I spoke them. Each time we finished, the judges' eyebrows went up and they scribbled something on their clipboards. Each time, one of them was grinning ear to ear.

During one of our breaks, a judge who taught physics at a college asked Ro a question. They started talking about dark matter and stuff I didn't have a single clue about, so I wandered off to look at some of the other projects. I saw Ping-Pong catapults and balloon-powered soda bottle cars and clocks that were powered by potatoes.

It was actually way cool.

After our last presentation, Ro and I just leaned against our table and sat in silence, because we'd done hours of talking. She put her windbreaker back on and took off her name tag. She pulled her hair back with her white hair tie. "So, where's your mom?"

"Home," I said.

"How did she . . ." Ro wouldn't quite look me in the eye. "You know. React?"

I looked down and shook my head. All last night, I'd been dreading the moment I'd face Mom. When I walked through the door Mom stared at me for a moment, as if she didn't recognize me. And then she sprinted across the hall and threw her arms around me, clutching me in a death grip and burying her face in my shoulder. "Oh, you're here," she said, her voice shaking, over and over again. "Thank God you're here."

And then after she'd taken a moment to collect herself, she sat me down at the table and wouldn't let me leave until

I told her every last thing; about how I'd found my dad through his comics and how I'd found out about his movie premiere. She interrogated me on how exactly I'd ridden my bike to the Greyhound station and then bought a one-way ticket to Los Angeles with my birthday money. And then when I told her about how I'd met Dad, her face paled and her lips pressed into a thin, flat line. I pulled out the napkin with his phone number on it, but she didn't even glance at it. And after I finally finished telling her every-thing, she was quiet. I noticed how dark her eye circles were. Her hair puffed out around her face; I could tell she'd spent the night nearly pulling it out.

The silence stretched on between us until Mom rose from the table, and, without speaking to me, turned and left.

Danny was the one who drove me to the science fair this morning. "How is Mom?" I asked.

Danny's hand tightened on the steering wheel. He let out a long sigh through his nose. "You shook her pretty bad. Running off like that. She was worried, Benji."

And that was all. I almost wished he would say some-thing more—that he would yell at me, or ask about Dad, or say *I told you so*, or tell me something, *anything*, that I could do to make this right, but he fell silent. I'd felt so awful that I practically wanted to evaporate.

But I totally, completely, one million percent deserved it.

And now here I was at the science fair, and with every passing minute I felt more and more guilty about what I'd done. "She's still a little mad. Okay, really mad." I shrugged. "I mean, I did run out on her. She'll talk to me sometime in the next decade or so, probably."

"I'm sorry," Ro said. "I'm so, so sorry I made you do this."

I glanced up. "Hey, fifty-fifty, remember? It's just as much my fault." I squared my shoulders. "Besides, we've got a science fair to focus on." I stood up. "Wanna see a Ping-Pong catapult?"

And so we went and looked at all the projects, wandering through the endless rows of poster boards before returning to our spot. At some point in the afternoon all the sleep we didn't get last night finally hit us. Ro got tired first and then I did. We almost fell asleep, leaning against our tables.

Until we were woken up by Ro's mom.

"Congrats!"

I bolted up. "Mmm-what? Did we miss something?"

"No," she said. "They're just starting awards right now. But you're done with science fair! I brought donuts." She waved a paper bag in front of our faces and looked around. "*Aiyah,* this place is huge."

Mr. Devlin hurried over. "They're announcing our categories now!"

"In third place is . . . Michael Banks and Lenny Goldstein from Buena Vista!"

"Want to go over?" Mrs. Geraghty asked.

"Hold on," Ro said through a mouthful of chocolate sprinkled donut. "Wanna finish this first."

256

"And in first place of the Northern California Regional Middle School Science Fair . . . Rosalind Geraghty and Benjamin Burns!"

Wait.

Hold up.

What?

Did they just—

"It's you!" Mr. Devlin shouted. "Go, go, go!"

We stayed frozen until Ro's mom said, "What are you waiting for?" We put down our half-eaten donuts and hurried toward the stage. Cameras flashed.

I really, really hope I didn't get chocolate frosting on my face.

They first placed the medal around my neck. As Ro walked up to the podium, her blue-and-white windbreaker billowed out behind her like a cape, and I swear, with the red medal ribbon around her neck, she kind of looked like Gemma Harris right then and there.

We turned. Cameras flashed, and the crowd burst into applause.

When I came home, Mom was sitting at the kitchen table, phone in hand.

"Hi, Mom," I said in a small voice. She glanced up but didn't reply. I was about to turn and head up the stairs when she said, "Benji."

I turned back.

"Come here."

I padded over and sank into the chair next to her.

"I just got off the phone with your father. "

I froze. "I'm so, so sorry," I burst out. "I know you probably never wanted to talk to him again and you're still probably mad at me for doing the whole running-away thing—"

"It's okay," she said. "He called for you, but you were still at the science fair, and then . . . he and I had a talk. A long talk, but a necessary one." She looked up. "Listen, Benji. I'm not saying that it was okay to do what you did. But you wanted to know who your dad was, and I never gave you the chance. And that was my fault."

She clasped her hands together. "Separating from your dad wasn't easy. I think about it all the time, you know. What things would have been like otherwise. I tried to raise you two just like every other kid on the block. But I know I couldn't make it the same. I know how much it affected you and Danny."

Mom used to joke to other people that she lived in scrubs. She'd always show up to Danny's games in them, because she'd rushed from her shift. How many times had she worked extra hours at the hospital just so she could afford a new mitt for Danny? Or my allowance?

She sighed. "I knew that questions about your dad and I would come up. I'd have to talk about it someday, but I always just got so upset thinking about it that I never wanted to. But you're growing up, Benji. Danny too. And I wanted to let you know that if you want to talk to your dad, I'm okay with that."

I nodded in relief.

"There . . . were a lot of good parts to your dad. He was a really talented artist. I see that in you. You should show me more of your art sometime."

She'd never said that to me before. I swallowed. "Yeah. I will."

"It's been a while since I've seen him." She sighed. "I think I forgive him a little more now. And guess what?"

I looked up. Mom looked like she was trying to hold back a smile. "What?"

She burst out, "He's paying for Danny's college!"

I stood up. "He is?"

"He better, now that he's making the big bucks!" She laughed. "But yes, he promised. And I'm supposed to get the first check by the end of next week." She grinned. "Now Danny can apply wherever he wants without having to get a baseball scholarship."

Mom had absolutely, positively never been happier.

I smiled. "Glad he's trying to keep his promises."

"Things are changing, for sure," she said. She leaned over. "But hey." She jabbed a finger in my face. "Next time you want to see your dad, give us all a heads-up instead of running off to the nearest Greyhound bus, will you?"

She held me at arm's length with a smile in her eyes.

"Because if you *ever* pull this again, I swear, you'll be grounded until you're fifty years old."

I laughed. "I promise I won't." Mom grinned and pulled me into a tight hug, still laughing. And crying a little, but mostly happy crying, I think.

Why had I ever thought my dad would be the super-hero? Mom had been standing in front of me all along, holding our world up on her shoulders.

CHAPTER THIRTY-FIVE
RO

AFTER THE SCIENCE fair, I went home and slept for twenty-two hours straight.

When I woke up the next day, it was late afternoon. I stumbled into the kitchen, rubbing my eyes with the palm of my hand. Mom was making tea and reading the mail. She looked up with an amused smile. "You don't normally sleep in so late. Tea?"

"Well," I said. "Things haven't quite been normal around here."

"You could say that again." Mom leaned forward, tucking her short black hair behind her ears. For once, she wasn't wearing makeup. "How are you feeling, baobao?"

She slid a mug over and I took it. I settled into a chair. The sunlight filtered through Mom's plants, casting ivy-shaped shadows on the counter. The chrysanthemum tea reminded me of my grandmother's apartment in San Francisco. "I'm all right," I said finally.

"The things I miss when I'm at work," Mom said, a smile in her voice. She stirred the loose tea flowers. "I get busy and all of a sudden I turn around and my kid's built a whole rocket. But that's not even the part that surprises me."

She leaned forward. "How on *earth* did Benji end up in Los Angeles?"

This was going to be a long story.

"When Benji and I first became friends, we made a deal," I said. "He would help me finish building my rocket, and I would help him find his dad."

And then I told her about *Spacebound*. How it was Benji's favorite comic book series. How Benji had found out that the person who wrote the series, was, in fact, his long-lost dad. How I'd found out about this after we got put together as science class partners and after our folders got accidentally switched. How we'd stumbled upon each other's secrets and made our deal; he'd help me with my rocket, and I would help him find his dad. How we came across clue after clue until we'd found the news of his movie premiere.

"And so I told him that maybe we could go see him," I said. The knot in my stomach was twisting tighter and tighter all this time. "And we had a big fight right before he ran away," I said. My voice rose. "It's all my fault, Mom.

262

I know it. I didn't make him go, but I got mad at him. He didn't want to go at first. I feel awful now but at the time I just was thinking—" I took a jagged breath. "I was just thinking that his dad was practically *right here* and that it was so easy for him to just go and see him if he wanted and *I* wished—"

I wasn't really making sense anymore. I buried my face in my hands. "I don't know."

Mom reached out and took one of my hands and squeezed it. "Baobao, I understand. Believe me, I understand."

I shook my head. "I almost ruined our friendship over this."

"But you didn't," she said gently. "And it's not all your fault. And even if you said anything, I'm sure he forgives you." She looked me in the eye. "You and Benji are such good friends. Even I can see it."

"You can?"

Mom nodded. I grinned down at the table.

We sipped our teas in silence for a bit. I looked at her plants on her shelves. Her English ivy vines were starting to cover parts of her brush paintings.

She finally said, with a hint of a smile, "So, you and Benji—"

"Mom."

"*Aiyah*, I was just wondering."

I didn't say anything. I mean, Benji and I were just

friends. Right? I knew how it felt to like someone. But not to *like*-like someone. What did that even mean? I thought of how I'd seen Danny and his girlfriend, Chelsea, when we ran into them at Vic's Ice Cream, how they leaned into each other and grinned all the time. Maybe it was that. But I'd also once heard from one of the girls at the Day School that when you liked someone your face turned bright red and your words just turned to mush every time you wanted to talk to them. I thought of my words turning to mush every time I tried to talk to Benji. That just sounded inconvenient.

Besides, how did kissing even work?

It was all too, too complicated.

For now, Benji and I were just people who split milkshakes and paid for each other's fries, who would drive all the way to Los Angeles to rescue the other from their dad's messed-up movie premieres. Who built rockets together and read comic books and shared Red Vines and told each other everything.

"Friends," I said, leaning back in the chair. "We're just friends," I said, as if it were the best thing in the world.

Which it was.

Mom nodded. She stirred her last bit of tea. "I just wanted to know," she said. "I feel like I've been so caught up in my work that I haven't had a good chat with my kid for a while." She paused. "You know I'm so very proud of you, right? Dad would have been, too."

I nodded. I didn't say anything for a while. "I won't ever stop missing him, will I?"

She paused. Her expression changed, and she reached for me, and folded me into a hug. I heard her cratered heartbeat through her shirt.

"Oh, love." She sighed. "You and me both."

I finally approached Drew one day after class as we both were walking to lunch. He saw me coming and tried to shift directions, but I had already stopped in front of him.

"Hey," I said, and he looked up at me reluctantly.

I cleared my throat. It occurred to me that this was the first time that Drew and I were, in fact, speaking face-to-face since the slime incident. But after all, it did seem like he'd been avoiding me since the science fair. "You cleaned the poster up, didn't you?"

He didn't say anything. He just shrugged.

"I just had a feeling you did. I don't know why. Maybe you didn't. We ended up having to make a new one, anyway, so I guess it wouldn't have really mattered in the end." I took a deep breath. "But I just wanted to say thanks anyway. If you did. It meant a lot."

Drew's expression softened. But still, he didn't say anything.

"See you around, I guess." I turned to go.

"Congrats, by the way."

I turned around. "What?"

He met my eyes with just a tiny hint of a smile. "On the science fair, smarty-pants. I heard." And when he said *smarty-pants,* it almost sounded like a compliment.

He turned and walked away.

CHAPTER THIRTY-SIX
BENJI

I SAT IN front of the phone, smoothing down the folded napkin from the diner in Los Angeles. I'd pulled a chair from the dinner table up to the kitchen counter and heard it creak as I sat up in it. I picked up the phone. I double- and triple-checked the numbers before I dialed them with shaky fingers.

What if my dad wasn't there? What if he was stuck in traffic coming home from someplace? What if he gave me the wrong number and I was dialing some random person in Los Angeles? And then he'd move and I'd never see him again—

"Hello?"

I slumped back in relief.

"Um, hi," I said. I cleared my throat. "Hi, Dad."

Cripes, it sounded *so weird*. I'd spent years dreaming

about just this moment. And now I could hardly bring myself to call him Dad.

"Hi, Benji." It felt strange to hear his voice right next to me and not be able to picture him. Where was he? Was he, too, at the kitchen counter, stretching the cord on the phone? Was he looking out over the Los Angeles skyline? Was he dressed up in a fancy suit, off in his studio, surrounded by colored pencils and markers and drawing paper? I could imagine it: the bright lights shining down upon him and the slabs of paper, the mess of acrylic colors on his desk. Because of course his desk would be messy. "I was hoping you'd call."

I nodded, and then realized he couldn't hear it over the phone. "Yeah. I wanted to."

A pause. "How are you doing, kid?"

I swallowed. "I'm . . . doing okay, I guess. Just kinda busy." I racked my brain for something, *anything*, to say. "Mostly science fair stuff with Ro."

"I thought science fair was three weeks ago?"

"Ro and I qualified for the state fair. It's in a few weeks."

"Oh, wow," he said softly. I could hear the grin in his voice. "Looks like you guys made it on time after all."

"Yeah," I said. "That was a crazy night."

"I bet it was." Another pause. "And how's your mom and brother doing?"

"Good," I said. "Mom's working as always. She seems a little happier now, though. And Danny's doing great. With baseball and all." I paused. "I gave him your number, too. I don't know if he's called you yet."

When Mom had told Danny about Dad pitching in for college during dinner, he'd scowled a little bit and pushed his fork around the pasta Mom had made.

Mom had looked at him. "I know that things have been complicated with him, but we should be grateful that your father's helping out."

He set his fork down. "He should have been helping out a long time ago." And then he didn't say anything for the rest of dinner. There seemed to be a wall that Danny had built up between him and Dad. We all knew. Even Dad could tell.

"He'll come around to it." Dad sighed. "If he wants to."

This time there wasn't just a small pause. The silence stretched on. My neck prickled with sweat. How did this room suddenly feel so warm? I could almost feel the walls closing in. My throat got tighter. It was *that* feeling again. The feeling when you were in an elevator with a stranger and couldn't find a single thing to say.

Except this stranger was my father.

It wasn't *supposed* to feel like this. We'd met. We'd made up. We'd already had a long talk in Los Angeles. It was supposed to get easier from then on. When did the inside jokes start coming? The conversations on the way to picking up burgers and shakes at a drive-through?

What if it would never get easier?

"Benji?" my dad said from the other side of the phone. "You still there?"

"Yeah," I said. "Sorry. I guess this is . . . kinda hard for me. I don't know."

He didn't talk for a while. My palms were clammy. What if Dad just gave up? Hung up the phone?

What if we never talked again?

"I know it must be hard," Dad said, exhaling. "I know things . . . aren't going to be the easiest. We haven't seen each other for years. I didn't reach out when I should have."

I nodded. "Yeah."

"But it's good to talk," Dad said. "I've dreamed about this for a long time. I hope we can still try to . . . have these calls. Even if it's difficult. And maybe things will get better over time." He paused. "That is, if you want."

I had to take small steps. But they were steps nonetheless.

I cleared my throat. "Yeah. I do."

"And I would love to see you again, too."

"Yeah. That would be kinda neat." I took a deep breath. "How's the movie coming along?"

I could almost hear him relax. "Oh, it's doing just fine. It's amazing seeing all those billboards, you know. Kind of out of this world. I'm still trying to wrap my head around it. But I guess now that the movie's premiered and all that, I'm focusing on sketching out the next issue."

I perked up. "Are we going to find out the secret of the alternate universes? Or Woz's origin story?"

"What do you think? Got any ideas?"

I was floored.

"Are you asking . . . for my ideas on the next issue of *Spacebound*?"

"Why not? Can't promise I'll use all of 'em, but I'm definitely all ears."

I grinned. But then a thought occurred to me. "Actually . . . I'll let you surprise me with this issue. I can't wait to read it."

He laughed. "Sounds good, Benji."

"But . . ." An idea had come to me. A crazy, out-of-this-world idea. "Let's say I was thinking about making my own comics. Got any pointers?"

"Of course," he said. "I'd love to help."

He was right. This wasn't going to get easy anytime soon. But the weight on my chest was letting up. We were talking. And for now, I was okay with that.

CHAPTER THIRTY-SEVEN
RO

AT THE STATE science fair in May, so many people came up to our table that some were craning their necks to get a look at our poster board. Adults dressed up with fancy jackets and name tags pored over every inch of our project. They passed around the rocket and scribbled things on their clipboards and asked us all kinds of questions. They closely inspected the airframe and fin designs. They seemed especially fascinated with the radio transmission system.

"It's like a satellite," some college professor said. "They're doing a lot of things with that now, NASA and the government. They're trying to put together a map of the world with satellite signals so you can know where you are in the world at all times. Like a virtual atlas. And there's another satellite project that's trying to look for extraterrestrial life."

Benji looked up. "Say what now?"

I grinned and turned to answer another question.

"You'll never believe this," Benji said excitedly when we were on break. "Rumor is there's an *actual* place that's opening up this year that's built just for looking for aliens. And *get this:* it'll be right near San Francisco!" He stuffed half a sandwich in his mouth. "I can't believe I'm saying this, but this space stuff is actually pretty cool sometimes."

I laughed and took a sip of Dr Pepper. "Who even are you anymore? What happened to the real Benji?"

"Taken over by an alien, actually. There's a faulty chip in the back of my neck. You have forty-eight hours to remove it or the entire planet is in danger."

I rolled my eyes. Benji was back again. "It's nice to see you nerd out over something other than comics for once."

"Hey," he interjected. "Not a nerd."

"Two more months and you'll be answering questions in class."

"You'd have to wake me up first."

The thing was, Benji actually paid attention in class sometimes. He still doodled in his notebook, but I rarely had to wake him up. I, on the other hand, had started hiding issues of *The Flash* under my notebook in class. At first, it was a little hard to believe—how could someone survive lightning and then develop superpowers?—but I had to admit, I was hooked. Now, I was through the first two volumes, and the scribbles and doodles from the corner of Benji's notebook had spilled over to mine.

"You know," he said. "The new *Spacebound* issue comes out today."

"Will you get it?"

Benji shrugged. "Yeah, eventually. I mean, I still read the series. I like it a lot. I'll probably read just to find out what happened to Gemma's spacepup. But after meeting my dad I went back to them and . . . I just wasn't obsessed with them anymore. Is that weird?"

I shook my head. "Not at all."

"I've been reading a lot of *X-Men* now," he said. "I wanted to read some other stuff. But I'm starting to talk to my dad some, so that makes up for it."

"Yeah, you'd mentioned," I said. "How's that going?"

There was a tentative smile. "Getting better, I think."

"That's good, I guess." I straightened up and checked my watch. "Awards are soon. Should we call everyone back in here?"

Benji looked around the room. "Yeah. Our moms are probably looking at the high school stuff. And Danny—" He froze. "Wait a second."

I followed Benji's line of sight right down to the guy walking down the row toward us. He came right up to our table, put his hands in his pockets, and smiled.

"Hey, kid," David Allen Burns said. "Surprise."

We didn't win the California State Science Fair. We got third.

But still, when the judges announced our names, and everyone clapped, and Mom and Benji's mom and dad cheered like crazy, and Mr. Devlin looked like he'd faint from happiness, I looked out from the podium and thought, *It doesn't get better than this.*

Except it did.

Because after we were handed our medals, Mr. Devlin pulled Benji and me aside.

"So people have been talking about your rocket," he said. A smile spread across his face.

Benji and I exchanged looks.

"Some people from the NASA Ames Research Center were there," he said.

"*The* NASA?" Benji asked incredulously. "Like . . . the one that sent people to the moon?"

"The one and only," Mr. Devlin said. His cheeks were bright red with excitement. "They have a base in the Bay Area. The folks over there loved your experiment. They said you two should seriously think about a future in this kind of stuff."

My heart dropped into my stomach.

It was all we could talk about when we went out to Vic's. I ordered my usual strawberry milkshake. Benji looked over at me. "Come on," he said. "Not gonna celebrate with a little extra?"

I shrugged. "I know what I like."

"I guess so," he said. And then he picked up the menu

and ordered the deluxe sundae, toppings and all.

All of us ended up staying hours at the ice-cream shop. Benji's older brother, Danny, came by, still in his baseball uniform and everything. He'd brought his girlfriend, Chelsea, and they squeezed into the booth that wasn't quite meant to fit seven people but managed to anyway. It was the first time I'd talked to either of them. Chelsea wore big hoop earrings and had her blond hair pulled up into a ponytail, and Danny had an easy smile and eyes just like Benji's. Danny ordered a vanilla milkshake and told us that he could drink milkshakes in under a minute, and when we dared him to, he downed the whole thing, leaving him with a goofy lopsided whipped cream mustache. We all laughed at him. Chelsea shook her head, but she was smiling, and then she leaned her head on his shoulder.

As I was finishing my strawberry milkshake, I realized that Benji's entire family was together, finally. I mean, sure, cramming them all into one booth might not have been the best idea. And I couldn't tell if Danny was ignoring their dad, or if he was just super-focused on his girlfriend. But the whole time, Benji was grinning from ear to ear. And my heart swelled up in my chest in this good and inexplicably painful kind of way.

"It was really great, seeing them all together like that," I told Mom at dinner, over our bowls of rice. "Benji was really happy."

Mom smiled. "I saw."

"He's been talking to his dad lots now. He even invited us to come visit LA sometime this summer. Wouldn't that be amazing? Benji and I are making a list of all the things we have to do once school's out."

Mom paused before looking down. "Actually, I wanted to talk to you about that."

"About LA?"

"No, about this summer," she said. "I just got off the phone with your grandparents."

"Is everything okay?"

"Yes!" Mom said sharply. "I mean, yes, of course. They're fine. We were just discussing . . . our future." She didn't quite meet my eyes. "And we talked for a long time and I was thinking that maybe . . . it's best to be closer to them." She shifted in her seat. "As in, live closer to them."

The happiness dissipated from my chest.

"So . . . we're moving?"

"Baobao, it would be a good way to start over and settle down for real," Mom said. "And I thought you've always loved the city." She paused. "And I know you and Benji are good friends, but you won't be far from him."

But we wouldn't be a three-minute bike ride from each other's houses.

"What do you think?"

I loved visiting San Francisco. I loved seeing the fog roll over the Golden Gate Bridge and driving through winding hills. I loved going to all these different restaurants and trying chicken and waffles one day and mochi the next. I loved going to my grandparents' favorite dinner place in Chinatown, where we'd sit around a huge circular table and try everything on the rotating platters and see Dad's face turn bright red after he ate anything with spice in it.

But I'd never truly imagined living there, because moving meant I would have to leave this place.

Moving to San Francisco meant leaving the place where Dad and I would look for meteor showers from the back of his truck. We'd leave behind the breakfast diner I'd been going to all my life with my favorite strawberry milkshakes in the world.

"I know you miss him," Mom said, as if she'd read my mind. "Just because we're leaving doesn't mean we'll stop missing him. But I want us to be surrounded by family. It'll help us heal, maybe just a little bit."

I thought of the boxes of Dad's stuff that had stacked up around the house, untouched for months. I thought of the times Mom had sat at the dinner table, staring at the painting Dad had gotten her; I thought of all the potted plants and the vines of English ivy that she'd bought in the months after That Night, that she'd carefully cultivated until they spilled across the kitchen, as if she were desperately trying to breathe some kind of life back into the house. I thought of the times I heard her crying, softly, behind her closed bedroom door.

Maybe, just maybe, moving to San Francisco would be the Next Best Step.

I couldn't look her in the eyes. "I have to think about it."

She nodded, chewing her lip. "Okay." Her eyes softened. "Thank you, baobao."

Leaving Sacramento also meant leaving my best friend, and that thought bothered me more than I thought it would.

CHAPTER THIRTY-EIGHT
BENJI

IT WAS WEIRD, not having a mission. I mean, I'd spent pretty much my entire life missionless. And Ro and I still hung out after school, and then after school let out, we called each other in the mornings and met up anyway. Sometimes we went over to Vic's and got huge waffle cones; I mixed it up every time, and Ro consistently got strawberry. We walked along the river until it got too hot and the ice cream dripped down our fingers. But most days, we biked over to Hogan's and still read comics. I caught up on the latest installment of the *X-Men* series. Ro had moved on from *The Flash* to *Wonder Woman*. We'd found out that Mr. Voltz was planning on taking a cross-country road trip with his dog.

"It'll be like what John Steinbeck did," he said, while he was tidying up the register.

I stopped inspecting the candy shelf. "Who's John Stein-beck?"

"He's a famous author," Ro said, finally looking up from her comics. "Right, Mr. Voltz? My mom reads some of his stuff. He took a road trip with his dog and wrote about it. Can we help plan out your trip?"

Still, it was weird to go home and do *nothing* again. And as school got out and the summer days got sticky-hot, Ro practically peeled me off the carpet of her house and told me we had to do *something*.

And that was how we ended up at the state fair. I hadn't been in years, but it was pretty much how I remembered it. There were white tents and colorful rides. I could smell the corn dogs and funnel cakes from the other side of the fairgrounds. The sun was hot on the backs of our necks and made our shirts stick to our skin.

I guess some things were better this time around. They'd added new rides with flashing lights. Danny had driven Ro and me here, so I could stuff my face with as much cotton candy as I wanted without Mom hovering over my shoulder.

Plus, I was completely crushing Ro at the carnival games.

"It doesn't make sense," she said as I beat her at another round of balloon darts. "Somehow my angles are always wrong."

"Angles don't cut it." I shrugged. "It's all about instinct."

"Okay, teach me."

"Not until I beat you another round."

"Well, you're being awfully secretive lately."

"Nuh-uh." I leveled my dart and closed one eye to aim. *Pop.*

"Yeah, you are. You won't even show me what you're drawing these days."

"Hey, that's a top-secret project," I said, turning to her. "I'll show you first, I promise. Even before I show my dad."

"Huh," she said. "You show him stuff now?"

"Sometimes," I said. "I mail him some of my drawings. He sends me some of his sketches for *Spacebound*, even before they publish it. We call sometimes, too."

Ro grinned. "That's good to hear."

"Yeah." I smiled at my shoes. "He's coming to visit us the weekend before school starts. Says he's going to take us down to Disneyland. You wanna come?"

Ro's expression froze. "I don't know."

"Come on," I said. I launched another dart. "It'll be our last weekend of fun before eighth grade starts. I heard all the homeroom teachers are super boring this year."

She wouldn't quite meet my eyes. She didn't say anything for a moment. Then, "I'm not coming back for eighth grade."

I stopped playing. "What?"

"I was going to tell you earlier, but I didn't know if anything was happening for sure or if we would sell the house but"—she took a deep breath—"we did. A week ago, actually. So yeah. We're moving to San Francisco at the end of this summer."

Wait.

What?

Ro Geraghty was *moving*. To a whole other city.

It was as if my heart had dropped into my stomach. *Whoosh.*

I didn't know what to say for a few moments. "That soon?"

Ro nodded.

"Oh."

"Yeah."

I looked down at the ground. I mean, I guess San Francisco wasn't too far away. Two hours by car, tops. I could even probably bike there in a day. Not that I ever would, but it wasn't like she was moving to Connecticut or something. Still, it was hard to think of her not being a three-minute bike ride from my house.

"You can visit me," she said. "When I move in. There's tons of places I can take you."

"Yeah," I said. "I will. And I'll write you."

"You better."

Ro's arms were crossed. I couldn't tell if she was sad or excited or over the moon about this, to be honest. For the first time, I couldn't read her expression.

She sighed. "I just . . ." She scrunched up her face, like she was trying to think of what to say. "It took me a long while to agree to it. I love the city. My entire family is there. From my mom's side, anyway. But I'll have to start all over again. I'll have to go to a new school where I won't know anyone. I was kind of mad about it at first, but I've kind of come to terms with it. I don't know. This could be good for us, maybe, in the long run."

"You'll be all right," I said. "You'll probably meet some cool people in the city." I smiled a little. "I'll be replaced."

"You're right," Ro said sarcastically. "Guess I'll just have to find another comic-book superfan with a secret famous dad to be friends with."

"Hey, you don't know," I said. "The odds could be pretty good."

"Anyway," she said, looking at the ground. "I'm still around for a few weeks. At least." She looked up. "Wanna try that?"

I looked at where she was pointing. It was a carnival ride that was shaped like the top part of a funnel. It was one of those newer rides that were painted with bright colors, with lots of flashing lights and *THE GRAVITRON* spelled out in neon letters.

"I've heard of these things before," she said. "I heard that the centrifugal force is so strong that you're practically glued to the wall."

"Let's do this," I said, even though I had no idea what on earth centrifugal force was.

We got inside and leaned back against the walls.

"I heard people try to turn upside down in these things," Ro said.

"Bet you can't," I whispered.

"Oh, you're so on."

Sure enough, the machine started spinning, slowly at first, and then faster and faster. My arms started feeling like lead. Ro tried to turn herself upside down on the wall, but the force was too strong, so she ended up in a weird position with her head leaning on my shoulder. And as the ride spun even faster and the lights blurred in front of me, Ro started laughing and her ponytail flew into my face, and despite the crushing weight, I couldn't stop laughing, either.

When we coasted to a stop, we were so dizzy that we almost fell over each other trying to walk out. Ro turned to me, her freckled grin wide and her hair messy and sticking up, like she'd stuck her finger in an electrical socket or something. "You're right," she said. "Couldn't do it."

"Told you."

"Come on," she said. "I bet I can kick your butt at the ring toss."

"Fat chance," I said.

I wasn't okay with Ro moving away. Not one bit. But I guess I always kind of knew that something like this would happen. Because the truth was, a place like this couldn't always contain her big grin and her crazy smart ideas and her wild experiments. And I knew that wherever she ended up in the future—in San Francisco, or in a spaceship that traveled to the edges of the universe—she would be just fine.

CHAPTER THIRTY-NINE
RO

THERE WERE A lot of things I didn't know yet.

I didn't know the exact science behind the Gravitron ride and how it could make your limbs feel like they were a million pounds. I still didn't exactly know how to launch a space shuttle into orbit. I didn't know the exact rate at which the universe was expanding, or if aliens existed, or whether space and time differed across different galaxies. I didn't know if there were other solar systems with life on them, or if there were alternate universes, or if there was an alternate universe where my dad never collided with that car on the way back from Raley's. I didn't know if the fluttering feeling in my stomach when I accidentally leaned my head on Benji's shoulder was because of the ride, or if meant something different.

Because here's the thing about the universe: sometimes

it doesn't tell you all its secrets at once. Sometimes you have to spend years, decades, to answer a question you have. Sometimes you have to travel to the deepest of jungles or to the edges of space to figure things out. And sometimes you don't figure things out, but get one step closer.

Tonight, with the smell of funnel cakes in the air and live music playing from the speakers by the stage, and with Benji sticking out his cotton-candy-stained blue tongue at me as I beat him at the ring toss, I realized that maybe it was okay to not know any of those things for a while. For tonight, at least. Because I was sure I would eventually figure it all out.

EPILOGUE

September 3, 1984

Dear Ro,

It's Benji Burns here, reporting live from Sacramento, California.

Imagine this: disaster reigns. The water tower has burst. The clouds have turned dark, and storms are gathering on the landscape; the crops have wilted and died. The town is being taken over by mind-reading extraterrestrial creatures and the moon has disappeared—

Just kidding. Things are totally fine here. Everything is normal. Well, as normal as things can be.

I hope this is the first letter you've gotten in your new apartment. What's it like? Is it twelve stories up? Can you see the bay? Do you have an incessantly annoying neighbor under you who owns a hundred cats with suspicious motives? Are there a thousand honking cars? Does everyone drink coffee? Do you get lost? Actually, I know that you never would get lost because you'd always have a map on you. Please tell me everything.

Okay, I have something to confess. Everything really is normal here, except for the fact that it's kind of not because you're not here. School's started over here, and it's weird not having you as a lab buddy. Science class is going to be a lot less fun this year, even if I'll probably know what's going on now. I've started hanging out with Jimmy Katz some. You remember him from class, right? He's started coming over to my house some. But it's not the same. I don't have anyone to share my comics with, and my packets of Red Vines go so slowly now that you're not here to steal half of them. They'll probably expire and get moldy. Except probably not, because Mom says Red Vines are probably made of plastic and chemicals and Red 40 dye and will never decompose and make me grow fangs or something. But there's still no chance she'll get me to stop eating them.

It's weird that a year ago, I didn't even know who you were. But secretly, I'm kind of glad that we accidentally took each other's folders on the first day of school, even if we were a little weird to each other. Because I would have never accidentally-on-purpose found my dad if it weren't for you. Or built a giant rocket.

Because the thing is, you go and do impossible things. Everyone else likes watching TV and pulling whoopee-cushion pranks on substitute teachers or whatever, but you like building rockets. You like doing experiments and wondering about what lies beyond our solar system. Sometimes I think you're too much of a nerd. But you're also one of the coolest people I know, and I hope you never change.

And guess what? Mom said I could visit San Francisco in October sometime. I'm coming ninety miles to see you, which is not a long distance, but it sure seems like it is. I hope you take me to all the cool food places and Chinatown (I'm going to eat ten of those pork buns, I swear). And we'll visit all those cool buildings and I'll probably wander off and get lost, but it's okay, because you'll have a map with you and you'll find me.

Anyway—until then, I hope you enjoy this thing I made. It's a space story too, but this one has radioactive robots and evil mad scientists and all the things I wished were in comics I read.

See you soon,

Benji

P.S. Sorry about the aliens in the corner. Couldn't help myself.

I unwrapped Benji's project from the tissue paper and nearly dropped it.

Because it was a full, whole comic book, with pages and a cover. I flipped through the pages. I looked at the artwork sprawling across the pages and the dialogue bubbles inked out carefully, at the characters bounding across cities and the spaceships hurtling through galaxies.

The pages were colored in with incredibly vivid colors and fine pencil lines. I looked at the bold block letters and the carefully sketched expressions on the characters' faces, and knew without a doubt that this was Benji's work.

I flipped to the cover.

It was a figure against the backdrop of a rocket, the universe painted in dazzling hues of blue and purple and black, clouds and dust and stars inked carefully, the planet a beautiful mix of red and orange.

And the figure in the center, piloting the rocket . . .

She was *me*.

I could see her freckles, her spacesuit that closely resembled my windbreaker, a superhero cape flying behind her as the rocket shot for the stars. I could see her hands on the throttle of the rocket, a corner of her mouth quirked up into a confident smile. And printed carefully across the cover was:

Across the Galaxy: The Chronicles of Ro.

My cheeks hurt from grinning so hard. I ran my hands over the cover, unable to speak or cry or laugh. Words disappeared from my tongue.

It was perfect.

And on the top was a sticky note, with Benji's unmistakable scribble:

I've been reading about other people's superheroes all this time. I thought it was about time I drew one of my own.

ACKNOWLEDGMENTS

Endless gratitude goes to my fantastic team at Quill Tree Books. To Alexandra Cooper, for championing Ro's and Benji's stories with incredible heart, guidance, and wisdom. It is an honor to work with you. To Ji-Hyuk Kim, for creating the cover of my dreams. To Allison Weintraub, Rosemary Brosnan, Shona McCarthy, Erin Fitzsimmons, Cat San Juan, Vaishali Nayak, Emily Zhu, Jackie Burke, Patty Rosati, Mimi Rankin, Katie Dutton, and Maya Myers: You helped make this book into what it is today. Thank you.

To my absolutely inimitable agent, Jess Regel. You took a chance on a nervous sixteen-year-old and nurtured my career with kindness, patience, and whip-smart insight. I can never thank you enough and I am so very lucky. To Mike Nardullo, for helping get my books to amazing places.

To my dad, for believing in my dreams even before I did. I owe everything to you. To my mother, for your strength and wit and brilliance—you inspire me every day. To Justin, for always rooting for me and for just being an all-around fantastic sibling. You're the best.

To Katia, for endless support and love and phone calls, for putting up with my crazy stories over the years, for providing sharp and insightful feedback, and for being there for me from the very, very beginning. You are my lighthouse.

To Maya, for reading those first words and for your priceless insights and friendship. You first made me believe this manuscript could see the light of day.

To Andi—you are my forever Yoda. You are my voice of reason. Thank you for the years of emails and phone calls and for patiently guiding me back onto the path when I lost my way.

To Becca, Lucas, Conor, Matin, and Dori, for providing invaluable feedback and for helping me make this book into the best version of itself. To Paula and Dave, for putting up with my questions and for creating such a wonderful home away from home. To Maya, Dave, and Tori, for teaching me all about rockets and space. I am so grateful to you all.

The fourth edition of the *Handbook of Model Rocketry* by G. Harry Stine was an invaluable resource during the course of writing this novel; any scientific or engineering error is purely my own.

To National Novel Writing Month, for helping me write

so many manuscripts over the years—including this one.

To #the21nders debut group, for the wonderful community and for being there during the highs and lows of this wild year.

Libraries and librarians make the world go round. To the Northbrook Public Library, for always having such an amazing collection of books. To Mrs. Cronin, for fostering my love of reading and writing and for keeping the school library full. Thank you. You are amazing.

To the writing community: you raised me, and I owe you one. To Cam and Michael, for rejoicing and commiserating with me over the writing process. To Melody, for always being in my corner from the very beginning. To Marisa and Rosanna, for the early feedback and encouragement. To Karuna, for taking me under your wing. To Grace, for the wonderful writing coffee chats. To Ch1Con for showing me the ropes. To Katie, Cindy, and Pablo, for your kind words and blurbs. To Tiffany, Lily, CW, and the bloggers who have taken in this book and given it so much love. And to Tashie, Joelle, Rona, Jake, Rocky, and Miranda, for not only supporting but enabling my chaos. I love you all.

Endless thanks also goes to those who cheered me on and offered me love and support in this process. To Katherine, for always talking books. To Cate, for always being in my corner no matter what. To Gaby, for cheering me on. To Eghosa, for believing in me. To Maeve, for supporting me from afar. To Lauren, for your encouraging and hilarious presence. To Rachel and Pranavi, for being the lights of my life. To Vida, for the serendipity. To Peter, for keeping me laughing. And to Jack, Jacob, Avery, Nik, Mihir, and Jeremiah: I am indebted to you all.

And last, to the infamous eighth grade Wood Oaks Science Fair crew—thanks for the timeless inside jokes, camaraderie, and *October Sky* reruns.